mercy

mercy

REBECCA LIM

HYPERION
NEW YORK

First U.S. edition, 2011
First published in Australia in 2010 by HarperCollins Publishers
Australia Pty Limited

1 3 5 7 9 10 8 6 4 2
V567-9638-5-11060

Printed in the United States of America

Library of Congress Cataloging-in-Publication Data
Lim, Rebecca.
Mercy / Rebecca Lim.
p. cm.
Summary: Mercy, an angel, wakes up again and again in different bodies, trying to
earn her way back into heaven while being hunted for a crime she did not commit.
ISBN 1-4231-4517-8 (alk. paper)
[1. Angels—Fiction. 2. Supernatural—Fiction. 3. Kidnapping—Fiction. 4. High
schools—Fiction. 5. Schools—Fiction. 6. Mystery and detective stories.] I. Title.
PZ7.L6342Me 2011
[Fic]—dc22
2011004942

Text set in Sabon
Designed by Marci Senders

Reinforced binding

Visit www.hyperionteens.com

*To my husband, Michael,
who makes it all possible*

With love always

CHAPTER
1

There's something very wrong with me.

I can't remember who I am or how old I am, or even how I got here. All I know is that when I wake up, I could be any age and anyone, all over again. It is always this way.

If I get too comfortable, I will wake one morning and everything around me will have shifted overnight. All I knew? I know no longer. And all I had? Vanished in an instant. There's nothing I can keep with me that will stay. It's made me adaptable.

I must always reestablish ties.

I must tread carefully or give myself away.

I must survive.

I must keep moving, but I don't know why.

I am my own worst enemy; that much I've figured out.

You know almost as much about me as I do.

I look sixteen. Sometimes I even feel it.

Me? The real me? I'm tall. Though I only have a sense of that.

I'm pale, like milk, but I never get sunburned. Don't ask me how I know this, seeing as I don't seem to occupy any physical space at the present time, but I just know.

My hair is brown. Not a nice brown or an ugly one, just brown. It's weird, but it has no highlights. It's all the same color, every single strand straight, even and perfectly the same. It hangs down just past my shoulders and frames my face nicely, which is oval and okay, I suppose. I have a long, straight nose, lips that are neither too thin nor too wide, and perfect eyesight. I can see for miles, through sunshine or moonlight, rain or fog. Oh, and my eyes? They're brown, too. And I never feel the cold, ever.

When I look in the mirror, I see this face—*mine*, I have learnt to recognize it, a palimpsest of a face, a ghost's face—within another's, a stranger's. Our reflections coexisting. I am her and she is me, and we, together, inhabit the same body.

How is this possible? I do not know. We are two people with nothing in common, nothing that ties us together, except that I am currently the reason *she*—whoever she is—can talk and move and laugh, go through the very motions of her life. I am like a grave robber, a body snatcher, an evil spirit. And she? My zombie alter ego who must do as she is told.

If I think hard about myself, really hard, I get the one word: *Mercy*. It's what I've taken to calling myself for want of something better. It might even actually *be* my name, but your guess is as good as mine.

My only real solace? Sleep. In the absence of an explanation for anything, for everything, I live for it and what it can bring.

Though I seem continually reborn, in this fogbound life I still have a kind of compass, a touchstone. He reminds me to call him *Luc* and appears to me only in my dreams.

His features are more familiar to me than my own. For I have traced them in my head and with my heart, such as it is. And perhaps once—though memory can be a treacherous thing—even with my hands, when they were real, made of flesh and bone and blood and not of the insubstantial air.

He has hair of true gold, cropped close, with sleek, winged brows of a darker gold, pale eyes, golden skin. He is tall, broad-shouldered, snake-hipped, flawless as only dreams can be. Like a sun god when he walks. Save for his mouth, which can be both cruel and amused. He tells me not to give up, that I must keep searching, find him. That one day it will all make sense. And all this? Will have seemed merely a heartbeat. *An inconvenience.*

"I am only a little ahead." He laughs as we sway together on a narrow precipice, high above a desert valley floor, the whole sleeping world spread out before us. "A little ahead."

His hand is steady beneath my elbow. If he were not here, I would surely fall, and even in dreams, die. Though my true name always eludes me—like him, it is always just a little ahead—my fear of heights does not. Why this is, again, I do not know.

As always, Luc warns of others looking for me: his erstwhile brothers, eight in number. That if They find me, They will destroy me. And that save for him, They are the most powerful enemies one may have in this world.

"If They catch you," he cautions, "They will surely kill you. And that, my love, is no dream."

He whispers these awful-beautiful things with his familiar half smile, before light seems to bleed from him for an instant. Then he is gone.

I wake with his warnings in my ears.

I wake now, sitting upright in the back of a bus packed with screaming, gossiping girls in matching school uniforms.

As I look down at the gray and dark red weave of the skirt I am inexplicably wearing, I wonder what disaster I am headed for as I try to figure out who the hell I am supposed to be today.

CHAPTER 2

"Carmen? CARRRRRMEN!"

My ears ring with the word, with the operatically rolled *R*s, the sonic after-bite.

I lower my head sharply and peer through an unfamiliar fall of black, curly hair. Momentarily disoriented, I realize suddenly that it is *mine*.

The racket is emanating from a sharp-faced, pigeon-chested blonde hanging over the seat back diagonally across the aisle from where I am sitting. I press my knees and hands tightly together to stop them from shaking.

So today, I suppose that must be who I am. *Carmen.* And the thought that I am no longer *Lucy*, or *Susannah*, or even the one before, whose name I can no longer remember, but whose life I liked very much and could have kept on comfortably living, makes my world spin, my breathing grow dangerously fast. I can feel the color draining out of Carmen's face as I fight for control of her body.

Everything is suddenly too loud, too bright, dialed up by a thousand. Carmen's heart feels like it will explode in her chest—ours—and if it does, it will be my fault, and I will be forced immediately to quit her lifeless body and take residence—like a ghoul, like a vengeful *ifrit*—in someone else.

Really, I should know what to do by now. You'd think I've had enough practice. But it never gets any easier. Not in those fateful first few days and hours, anyway.

I force my breathing to slow, and focus with difficulty. The muscles of Carmen's neck, her face, refuse to do as they are told. I am drenched in sweat, sure that Carmen's features are flushed with a strange, hectic blood.

Whoever the blonde is, she can see my clumsiness, the sudden wrongness in Carmen's expression, her demeanor, because the blonde's look sharpens, her already shrill voice rises an octave, and she shouts,

"What's wrong with you today, you dopey bitch? Jesus, you've been acting really weird. Like, hello? Is anyone in there for, like, the *fifteenth* time? Don't you want to *know* who Jarrod Daniels is doing now?"

And the whole coach falls silent, every head turning our way.

Dopey bitch? With those two words I feel Carmen's heart kick into even higher gear, almost whining under the strain of my sudden, white-hot anger. I have a temper, then; that's interesting to know.

Inexplicably, my left hand begins to ache dully, and I cradle it inside my right elbow, against my side, as if I have been recently wounded. Carmen's skin is now so hot that I know for certain that if I allow this to continue, I *will* kill her. And she is innocent and that cannot happen. It is as if an edict has arisen in me that I am currently powerless to fulfill.

In the strange manner I sometimes have of taking in too much, too quickly, I register in a split second that there are nineteen other girls present, two teachers—both female; both on the wrong side of old; one with short, iron-gray hair, jangly earrings, and a hard face; another with a girly bob and meaty jowls—and a driver who is consumed by the black fear that his wife is about to leave him for another man. It hangs about him like a detectable odor, a familiar on his shoulder, gnawing at his flesh. Is it only me that can see it?

Then the world telescopes, narrows, grows flat, becomes less than the sum of its parts again. Carmen's heart slows, her breathing evens out. My left hand has ceased to ache, and I release it, sit straighter.

Still, every eye in the bus is turned on us. Are "we" friends? Who *is* she to me?

Still struggling to get Carmen's face under control, I slur, "Bad migraine."

In my last life—well, Lucy's—I got migraines all the time. For someone like me, who doesn't feel the cold and never gets sick, not the essential *me* anyway, it had felt like intermittent war breaking out in my head. As if Lucy's mind and body kept finding ways to turn on me, determined to finish me off. I don't miss being Lucy, though I wish her well and hope she's recovered from my casual trampling upon her life. No doubt, in time, I will forget her, too.

My weak response is enough to satisfy them all, because eyes swing away uninterestedly, the noise level in the bus climbs back up to a jet-engine roar in my ears, and the sharp-faced blonde snaps, "That's *so* retarded," before turning huffily to speak to somebody else and leaving me blessedly alone.

Like a facsimile of a human being, I turn awkwardly to face the window and discern farmland flying by beneath an iron sky, punctuated by dead trees and storage areas, the occasional chewing cow, ordinary things, the grass by the roadside growing taller and coarser the farther we travel. Red soil gives way to sandy patches, vast stretches of salt plain. I imagine I can smell the sea, and wonder where we are. Not Lucy's domain of smelly high-rises and disgruntled dope dealers on skateboards. Not Susannah's toney mansion with the round-the-clock, live-in help and the hypochondriac mother who would never just let her *be.*

The land is as dry as Carmen's eczema-covered skin. Without having to think about it too much, I scratch urgently at the rough patch near her right wrist until it begins to bleed steadily onto the cuff of her long-sleeved white shirt.

Some things, I've found, the body simply remembers.

We finally pass a sign that says, WELCOME TO PARADISE, POP. 1503. Beyond it, a hint of dirty gray water, white caps rolling in the distance.

The name causes a little catch in my breathing, though I can't be certain why. I do not think I have ever been here before, in the way that I can sometimes recall things, impressions really; sixteen, thirty-two, forty-eight lives out of context.

Perhaps the town's misguided civic optimism is something that amuses Carmen. For I get flashes of my girls, my hosts, my vessels, from time to time. They are with me, but quiescent, docile. Maybe they believe they are dreaming and will shortly awaken. Some do occasionally make their way to the surface— like divers who have run out of air, breaking above the waterline clawing and gasping—before simply winking out because the effort is too great to sustain. It makes things only marginally easier that there is not a constant dialogue, a rapprochement, between us. Still, I am very aware that I occupy rented space, so to speak, and it informs everything that I do, everything that I am. I am never relaxed, because I am never wholly comfortable inside a skin that is not mine.

It is so far from it, Paradise, this small, dusty town laid out in a strict grid and set down on the edge of a peninsula, nothing pretty about it and seems to just peter out into the ocean. The high school we pull into—all low, boxy buildings, cyclone fencing and endlessly painted-over graffiti—sits on the town's barren outskirts, making no attempt to blend in with the landscape.

The bus shudders to a halt, there is a hiss as the front door releases, and a restive ripple of movement from the people around me, like an animal stirring.

I have not spoken for over an hour, not having trusted myself to form the appropriate words. When someone snaps impatiently for the second time, "Carmen Zappacosta," it is only the blond girl's loud, derisive snort that has me raising my head slowly and then my hand. When I let it fall again, it hits my lap with a dull sound, like dead flesh.

I narrow my eyes. It is the teacher with the gray hair and hatchet face speaking. She shakes her head before continuing sourly, "House rules are no drinking, no smoking, no sleeping with any member of the host family. Over the years of this little 'cultural exchange' program, we've had stealing, people going AWOL, emergency hospitalizations, immaculate conceptions. Wrongdoers *will* be dealt with ruthlessly. And try to remember why it is that you're here—as representatives of St. Joseph's Girls' School. You're here to *sing*, and that is *all*. Am I clear, or am I clear?"

The bus is a sea of rolling eyes as people rise excitedly to get their things. I watch to see what remains and then take it, stumbling after the others as if the bus is a pitching sailboat.

On the way out, I catch the driver's eyes—like burning holes beneath his meticulous comb-over—and he sees that somehow I *know*, because he looks away and will not look at me again, even though I stare and stare. Can no one else see it? That misery that envelopes him like a personal fog.

"Call me when you get over your little *episode*," hisses the frosty blonde over her shoulder as I fall down the stairs behind her under the weight of Carmen's loaded sports bag, almost landing on my new host father. I register that he is a strong-jawed, dark-haired man of unusual height dressed in khaki pants, a casual shirt, and dark blazer. Nice looking. What is the adjective I am looking for? That's right. *Handsome.*

I know he is waiting for me because I'm the last girl to get off the bus. All of the other girls are already shrugging off their blazers, letting their hair down, making eyes at their host brothers, checking out the situation.

"So this is Paradise!" I hear the blond girl exclaim flirtatiously.

If I were to be truly convincing, I should probably be doing the same, but I'm no good at flirting—there's no sweetness in me—and it is a simple triumph just to stand vaguely upright. I am aware that I am leaning slightly, and make appropriate but subtle adjustments to my posture.

The man Carmen has been entrusted to does not notice; he maintains his kind smile, his steady, patient expression. Neither does he notice the indefinable distance between himself and all the other people gathered in the parking lot. Eyes dart his way constantly, there is talk, talk, talk, mouths opening and closing, sly laughter, disapproval, but he does not see it. Or chooses not to. Instead, he takes Carmen's bag out of my dead grasp and shoulders it easily.

I follow him numbly, just putting one foot in front of the other; every step I take upon the surface of the world imprinting itself upon my borrowed bones.

14

CHAPTER 3

After stowing Carmen's bag in the trunk of his car, the tall stranger opens the front passenger door and gallantly sees me settled, before taking the driver's seat.

When he puts out his bearlike hand and says kindly, "Hello, I'm Stewart Daley," I must remind myself to do the same. Not observing the conventions can make you seem like an alien.

"Uh, hi, uh, Car-men, um, Zappa . . . costa," I mutter awkwardly, searching for the girl's name in my recently laid-down memory.

If he wonders why I'm having trouble pronouncing my own name, he's polite enough not to show it.

But the instant my hand meets his, I absorb a sensation like liquid grief, a kind of drowning. It is completely at odds with the man's friendly exterior and fills the space between us like floodwater surging to meet its level. A wild thing has suddenly been let loose in the car, a wordless horror, screaming for attention, and I cannot help but pull back as if the man is on fire.

Then the car's mockingly ordinary interior reasserts itself. I notice the leaf-shaped air freshener hanging from the mirror. The slightly smoky tint of the windshield. The leather bucket seats, faux wood-grain dash, the ragged road map in the passenger-side pocket. My breathing evens out, my left hand no longer burns with that strange phantom pain.

Whatever it is, this feeling, this horror, this secret, it lingers about him like a detectable odor, something gnawing at his flesh. I wonder that I didn't see it before, the man far more adept than the bus driver at hiding the cancer in his soul. It is only discernible through touch. Interesting.

"I suppose you've heard," he says, withdrawing his hand quickly. He looks away, blinks twice, before starting the car. "This is a place where everyone knows everyone else's business. They probably clued you in already. Can't say I blame them. I'd want that for my own kid."

We head out of the parking lot in the man's comfortable family wagon and head at determined right angles through the town, through the main street with its barbecue chicken shops, mini-marts, laundromat, family diners, bars. We don't speak again until he stops the car outside a white-painted, double-story, timber family home with prominent gables, a two-car garage, picket fence, bird feeders on the lawn. The place is neat, well maintained, like the man himself.

Unlike its neighbors, the house comes complete with three giant guard dogs—Dobermans—all sleek black-and-tan muscle. Two lie across the footpath to the front door, the other on its back on the lawn, all three languid and deadly. Something about their presence tugs at me, won't come clear.

"You'll want to stay in the car a moment," Mr. Daley says gently.

He gets out and engages in an elaborate ritual of unlocking a heavy-looking chain and padlock setup he's got going on his front gates that would make visiting the Daleys a pretty interesting exercise. When he's finally swung the gates open, he slips through, whistling for his dogs to follow. But one suddenly lifts its head and breaks rank, then they all do. And without warning, they're through the gates and circling the car, snarling and barking. They scratch at the doors, snapping on hind legs, seeking a way in, a way to get to *me*. I feel Carmen's brow furrow, realize I am doing it. Then I remember.

Dogs, more than any other creature, sense *me*, fear *me*. Perhaps even *see* me trapped inside a body that isn't mine. Where I've recalled this from, when, escapes me. All I know is, it will make Carmen's time in Paradise a lot more complicated.

"Come!" Stewart Daley roars, perplexed when the dogs refuse to obey.

When they continue to ignore him, bent on somehow eating their way through the car door to me, he drags them away by the collar, one by one, and locks them behind a head-high side gate. The dogs continue to howl and froth and claw at the chain-link, barbed-wire-topped fence with their front paws as if they are possessed. It is a scene out of the horror movies Lucy used to live for, as if her own life weren't horrible enough.

"I'm sorry," Mr. Daley says, breathing heavily as he opens my car door. "I can't understand it. I mean, they bark from time to time. But that? Well."

I shrug Carmen's thin shoulders—easier than forming words of explanation—and get stiffly out of the car.

When he tries to put a hand on my shoulder to usher me into the house, I cannot stop myself from flinching away. I can almost feel the man's hurt as he moves ahead, still toting Carmen's bag.

But I'm grateful for the distance he's put between us. Several times, like someone in the grip of a dangerous palsy, an incurable illness, I trip over things that aren't there, and I'm glad he doesn't see it. The walk from the car to the house may as well be measured in light years, eons. I am perspiring heavily, though the day is overcast and very cool.

His wife suddenly appears at the painted white front door, and I stumble to a standstill. It is surprise that does it. Seeing the two of them together like—what is that saying?—apples and oranges.

"Carmen?" she calls out warmly. "Welcome, dear, welcome."

Mrs. Daley is an impeccably groomed woman who used to be very beautiful, and still dresses as if she were, with great care and attention to detail. But she has a secret, too, and it is eating away at her soul, has taken up residence in her face, which is all angles, lines, hollows and stretched-tight skin beneath her sleek, dark fall of hair. She wears her grief far less lightly than her husband does, or he is much better at dissembling. Whatever the reason, she looks to me like the walking dead.

I am completely unprepared when she surges out of the house and wraps one of my hands in hers. It is all I can do not to wrench myself away and flee—back past the killer dogs, the unlovely school, the bus driver whose still beating heart has already been removed from him. There is the sense that I am the only still point in a spinning, screaming world. What resides beneath her skin is a manifold amplification of the horror beneath her husband's.

I break contact hastily on the pretence of tying a shoelace and, mercifully, the noise, the shrieking, is cut off. She stands over me silently like an articulated skeleton in cashmere separates and pearl-drop earrings, and yet *all that* is happening beneath the surface of her, behind her eyes. What a pair they make. What kind of place *is* this? What am I doing here?

"This way, dear," says Mrs. Daley calmly as her

husband precedes us up the stairs to the bedrooms, Carmen's bag in hand.

He pushes open a white-painted door to the immediate left of the lushly carpeted staircase. It is clearly a girl's room, filled with girl's things—an overflowing jewelry box; posters of heartthrobs interspersed with ponies, whales, and sunsets; a dresser teeming with glitter stickers and photos of a very pretty blond girl chilling with a host of friends more numerous than I can take in. Popular, then. There's a single bed and cushions everywhere, one of which spells out the name *Lauren* in bright pink letters. Like the house, the room is neat and clean and white, white, white. I wonder where she is, this Lauren.

"I'm sorry that our son, Ryan, couldn't be here to greet you," Mrs. Daley says, shooting a quick look at her husband. Her skeletal hands sketch the air gracefully. "We've made some space for you in the wardrobe, and you can have the bathroom next door all to yourself. That was—"

Mr. Daley half turns toward the door, says quietly, "Louisa . . ."

His wife smoothly changes tack. "It's entirely free for *your* use, Carmen. There's a shower and a bath, hair dryer, toiletries. You'll find fresh towels in the shelves beside the sink."

I nod my head. "I might use it now, if that's okay with you, Mrs. . . . Daley, Mr. . . . Daley. It was a very long, uh, trip."

Little do they know how long. A whole lifetime away, a whole world.

My voice is rusty, hesitant. Accents on all the wrong places, accents where there shouldn't be any. Not the mellifluous voice of someone who is here to sing, not at all. I watch them warily, waiting for them to spot the one thing in the room that doesn't belong. But they notice nothing and withdraw gently, still murmuring kind words of welcome.

At least I'm looking forward to waking up here in the mornings. Every time I opened my eyes at Lucy's, I wanted to be someone else, somewhere else, so desperately that it *hurt*. So long as I don't let these people touch me again, maybe things will work out fine.

I finally remember to breathe out.

I wander around the bedroom and bathroom and wonder what's behind the other closed doors on the landing, all of which are painted white and identical.

After my shower, I study myself in the giant wall-to-wall mirror. If her busty, acne-plagued companions on the bus are anything to go by, Carmen is supposed to be nearing the end of high school, right? But she looks about thirteen, with thin shoulders, no curves to speak of, and arms and legs like sticks. Way below average height. Her head of wild, curly hair seems almost too big, too heavy, for her scrawny frame. Carmen's eczema is really severe, making her naked body look scarred and blotchy. Not a bikini-wearer, then. I can imagine her being a confidante of that bossy blonde on the bus only because she poses no threat to anyone whatsoever. Not in looks or popularity or force of will.

Within the girl's underwhelming reflection, I discern my own floating there, the ghost in the machine. Somehow weirdly contained, yet wholly separate.

"Hi, Carmen," I say softly. "I hope you don't mind me soul-jacking your life for a while."

I hear nothing, feel nothing; hope it's likewise.

Soul-jacking. That's my own shorthand for whatever this situation is. I mean, like it or not, they're kind of my hostages and I can make or break them if I choose to. It's just me at the wheel most of the time. It's entirely up to me how I play things, however fair that may seem to you, but I try to tread gently. Though in the beginning, when I must have been wild with confusion, rage, pain, pure fear? I am sure I was not so kind.

I'm back in Lauren's room, wearing only a white towel, when I hear a commotion on the stairs, a heavy, running tread. I hear Mrs. Daley shout, "Knock before you go in there, Ryan, for heaven's sake!" Then the door bursts open and I'm face to face with a young *god*.

Carmen's heart suddenly skids out of control at the instance of shocked recognition at some subterranean level of me, though I am certain that neither she nor I have ever met him before. Yet he seems so familiar that I almost lift my hands to stroke his face in greeting. And then it hits me—he could be Luc's real-world brother, possessing the same careless grace, stature, wild beauty. And for a moment I wonder if it *is* Luc, if he has somehow found a way out of my dreams; an omen made flesh.

Yet everything about the young man towering over me is *dark*—his hair, his eyes, his expression; all negative to Luc's golden positive. Like night to day.

No sleeping with any member of your host family.

I suddenly recall the words, and it brings a lopsided smile to my face. I mean, it wouldn't exactly be a chore in this instance. He's what, six feet five? And built like a linebacker angel.

Just my type, whispers that evil inner voice. I've always loved beautiful things.

"What the hell are you smiling about?" Ryan—it must be Ryan—roars.

Carmen's reaction would probably be to burst into noisy tears. But this is *me* we're talking about.

I look him up and down, still smiling, still wearing my towel like it's haute couture. The need to touch him is almost physical, like thirst, like hunger. But I'm afraid of getting burned again, and there's a very real possibility of that. There's a good reason I don't like being touched, or to touch others. It invites in the . . . unwanted.

So instead, I plant a fist on each hip and stare up at him out of Carmen's muddy, green-flecked eyes. "I was just thinking," I say coolly, "about what you'd be like in bed."

CHAPTER
4

Ryan rocks back on his heels. "I'm going to ignore what you just said and ask what the hell you're doing here!" he says after a shocked pause. "This bedroom is off-limits."

"Ry-an!" exclaims Mrs. Daley, who's just joined us and overhears the last part.

"*Ry-an,*" repeats his father, who moves to stand in front of me protectively. "Carmen is a *guest* in this house. We've talked about it. You know it's long past time."

What is he? I wonder, my eyes still fixed on Ryan in fascination. *About eighteen? Nineteen?*

I don't bother to engage with any of them because I'm still checking him out and no one can make me rush something I don't want rushed. I can be stubborn like that. I mean, life's too short already, and I haven't seen anyone who looks like Ryan Daley in my last three lives, at least. Luc aside—and there's really *no* putting Luc to one side—Ryan is quite spectacular.

When I continue to say and do nothing, Ryan turns and snarls in his mother's face, "She's still alive, you know, *alive*! What are you doing even letting her come in here? Have you both *lost* it?"

Then he's gone, followed swiftly by his father. The door slams twice in rapid succession and the house is quiet.

Mrs. Daley sits down shakily on the pristine bed while I quickly pull a T-shirt from out of Carmen's sports bag over my head and put some underpants on under the towel, before laying it on a chair to dry. Not that I care about the proprieties, but I can see that *she* does, that they are the only things keeping her from flying into a million pieces. I dig around in the bag a bit more and locate some jeans. They look like something a little boy would wear. I am amazed when they fit perfectly.

"Stewart says they told you," Mrs. Daley murmurs softly. "About us, I mean. Did they?"

I shake my head. But it's pretty clear to me that we have a missing girl on our hands and that it was someone's bright idea to assign me her bedroom. I'm not sure what to make of it, and neither is Carmen's face, so I blunder into the closet, pretending to look for something, while Mrs. Daley clears her throat.

"We haven't, ah, hosted anyone since our daughter, Lauren . . . went away," she says, then corrects herself in a tight, funny voice. "*Was taken.*"

I shoot her a quick glance across the room. Her eyes are bright red in her chalky face, and I'm afraid of what she'll do next. Emotion is such a messy thing, apt to splash out and mark you like acid. I look away, refocusing hastily on Carmen's sports bag, the motley collection of belongings that sits on top. Weird stuff she thought it important to bring—like a frog-shaped key ring and a flat soft toy rabbit, gray and bald in places, that has clearly seen better days. There's even a sparkly pink diary with a lock and key. Little girl's things to go with the little boy's clothes.

When Mrs. Daley's agonized voice grinds into gear again, I begin to unpack in earnest, putting Carmen's belongings, her religiously themed songbooks, into the spaces allotted for her in Lauren's closet.

"We're trying to . . . *normalize* things for the first time in almost two years," Mrs. Daley whispers to Carmen's profile. "We used to host students all the time. Lauren loved meeting people from your school. She has . . . *had*, I should say, a lot of Facebook friends from St. Joseph's."

"Oh?" I say. Do I know what a face book is? It rings no bells with me.

"Ryan," she continues, "is having trouble letting go. We've almost come to terms with . . . I mean, you never really stop wondering . . . if she suffered, what really happened, how we could have prevented it . . . but we— Stewart and I—don't think of her as being . . . *present* anymore, in the sense that you and I are. Though Ryan insists—despite all the evidence to the contrary—that she's still alive. It's become something of an obsession with him. He says he can still *feel* her. He's . . ." She hesitates and looks away. "He's been arrested a couple of times for following 'leads' no one else can prove. But it's impossible. There was a lot of . . . blood."

Mrs. Daley, eyes welling, is staring at something on the floor between us that I cannot see. I wonder what she used to get the carpets so white again.

"She must have put up such a fight, my poor baby. . . ."

The woman lets slip a muffled howl through the clenched fingers of one fist, and then she is no longer in the bedroom. A door clicks loudly along the hallway. I don't know why she bothered shutting it, because the

29

sound of her weeping rips through the upper story of the house like a haunting. Habit, I guess, the polite thing.

Only sinew, thread, and habit, I decide, is holding Lauren's mother together. *Maybe*, I think, *I won't enjoy waking up here in the mornings, after all.*

There's no discernible pattern to the Carmens, the Lucys, the Susannahs that I have been and become. All I know is that they stretch back in an unbroken chain further than I can remember—I can sense them all there, standing one behind the other, jostling for my attention, struggling to tell me something about my condition. If I could push them over like dominoes, perhaps some essential mystery would reveal itself to me; but people are not game pieces, much as I might wish it. And there is nothing of the game about my situation.

When I "was" Lucy, I was a twenty-six-year-old former methadone addict and a single mother with an abusive boyfriend. I think I left her in a better place than where she was when our existences became curiously entwined, but it has all become hazy, like a dream. I think, together, we finally booted the no-hoper de facto wife basher for the last time and got the hell out of town with the undernourished baby and a bag of barely salvageable items of no intrinsic worth. I still wonder how she's doing, and if she managed to keep clean, now and forever, amen.

And Susannah? She was finally brave enough—with a little push from yours truly—to get out from under her whining heiress mother's thumb and accept a place at a college a long, long way from home, but that's where the story ends. For me, anyway.

I wish them both well.

The other girl? The one whose life I ended up liking but whose name now escapes me? She finally came up with a reason to escape an arranged marriage, change her name, find work in a suburban bookstore and love at her new local pub—thanks in no small part to me.

I liked that part. *Love.* It was uncomplicated, sweet. So unlike my own twisted situation. But the details are fraying around the edges, and soon she'll be gone, like all the rest. Doomed to return only in prismatic flashes, if ever.

Carmen looks and acts a lot younger than her three predecessors. Apart from her unfortunate skin condition, she doesn't *appear* unhappy or abused in any way. She really does seem to be here just to sing. It's the family she's been placed with that has the terrible history. And that's something that's got me wondering. Memory is an unreliable thing, but this seems new to me—an unexpected twist, an irregularity, in the unbroken arc of my strange existence to date. It does not feel like anything I have ever encountered before, though I may be wrong. I'm going to have to watch my step.

Once I have the mechanics of someone's life under my control, the thought always returns—that maybe someone is *doing* this to me. That I am some kind of cosmic, one-time experiment. Maybe it is the so-called "Eight"? But then I wonder, are They even real? Is Luc? Perhaps someone *is* trying to teach me a lesson. But one so obscure I still don't know what I'm supposed to be learning.

The unpalatable alternative is that maybe I'm somehow doing this to *myself*, that I'm some sort of mentally ill freak with a subconscious predilection for self-delusion, impermanence, and risk. If that is the case —and I pray that it isn't—the real truth is that there would be nothing left to stop me from topping myself, I swear to God. I almost don't want to know the answer.

And you need to ask why I call myself "Mercy"?

CHAPTER 5

I have barely closed my eyes when he is with me again. My own personal demon.

But tonight there are to be no perfumed midnight gardens, no bleak rocky outcrops of strange and savage beauty or shifting desert landscapes beneath unbroken moonlight—scenes engineered to enchant and caress the senses; some kind of reward for past injustices meted out. It is just a swirling, buzzing dark with us two at its heart. I sense Luc is angry and I feel a stirring of faintly remembered . . . *fear*?

Even so, his golden presence sings through my nerves, makes me feel more alive than any substitute life ever could. I want to touch him as badly as I wanted to touch Ryan Daley, but he holds me apart from him effortlessly, without even moving.

"Of course I'm real," he retorts, as if we are continuing a conversation that started long ago. "Do not doubt that. And you know who's caused this. You've never been stupid, so don't start now. The knowledge is *in* you despite everything that's been done to you."

I know now that I have always been quick-tempered, and his words bring forth an answering fury as he continues to hold me away when all I want him to do is wrap me in his arms.

"You think I don't know that?" I spit. "That somehow I've misplaced my life, my *self*, somewhere? What more do you expect me to do, the circumstances being what they are?"

I do not like the whining note in my voice. It is unbecoming. I've always preferred to think of us as equals, even if he *is* a long-standing figment of my diseased imagination.

He laughs, the darkness ringing with genuine amusement, and his anger subsides, though he moves no closer. He still holds us apart as if he were a being of pure energy.

"I *expect* you to do nothing as it concerns your . . . hosts"—he smiles—"and yet everything to do with finding me. So far, you've failed. You've got everything the wrong way around."

I frown. That may be, but how else am I supposed to survive the Lucys, the Susannahs, even the Carmens? Some of their existences are like little hells, and yet I am supposed to endure them *as they are*?

"But that's just it," I snap, and in the cold dark my left hand aches again with that inexplicable pain. "I don't know how to find *me*, so I sure as hell don't know how to find *you*. And anyway, I'm not even certain you're worth it any more." This last said to wound.

His beautiful mouth curves up in a half smile. My hand aches harder. I'm lying, of course—he's the very core, the heart, of my floating world, my floating life—but it still feels good saying it. I was not always this defiant with him, and I sense surprise, displeasure beneath the diverted expression.

"*Do nothing*," he says again, "and in doing so, find me."

There is a loud crack, like thunder, and I wake alone in Lauren's pristine bed. The fierce dawn winds blow great sheets of grit through the parched streets and gardens of Paradise like a parody of rain, like the feeling in my borrowed heart.

"So how was it?" says the rat-faced blonde from the bus in her hard-as-nails voice.

We're at the first collective Monday morning choir rehearsal of our two-week "cultural exchange" with Paradise High. It's supposed to culminate in massed, youthful voices belting out Part One of Mahler's Symphony no. 8 in E-flat major to an appreciative audience of local farmhands, fishermen, small-business owners, and parents. I only know this because I spent an hour last night after a tense dinner with the Daleys senior —Ryan's absence itself a presence—flicking through Carmen's belongings for clues as to what she was meant to be doing here. The piece is a pretty big demand, given that most of the students seem to be here under some form of duress and a good number of them are likely to be tone deaf. Plus, we seem to have misplaced an entire, uh, symphony orchestra somewhere.

One thing I'm sure of: Mahler is definitely not for sightseers. Carmen's score is dense with her own handwritten notes and symbols I don't even recognize. I'd way lost interest in it long before I'd even figured out where the choir's supposed to come in. Proposed course of action? Just pretend to sing for the next two weeks and hope no one notices. I figure it can't be too hard to lose yourself in a crowd.

And it *is* a crowd. It's eight in the morning and there are more people gathered in the assembly hall than I would have expected. Paradise doesn't look like it could possess fifty reasonably musical offspring, let alone the roughly two hundred teenagers I see here, checking each other out brazenly. It's like a meat market, and Carmen's group is giving as good as it gets. The air is practically sizzling.

"Are you having another mental attack?" says Ratface suspiciously when I don't answer her right away.

I dart a look at the cover of her score, which bears the name *Tiffany Lazer* in a cloud of hearts and flowers. It suits her. It's fluffy and deadly, at the same time.

"Nope," I reply casually. "Just scoping out the, um . . . hotties, uh, Tiff."

It's the right thing to say, because Tiffany relaxes immediately. "Speaking of which, so how was it? I hear

Ryan Daley looks all male-modelly super-gorgeous but is pretty much a psycho, nut-job disaster waiting to happen. I was *soooo* jealous at first when I found out who you'd got, but now I'm so glad it's not me! You're practically in the middle of an ongoing murder investigation—how twisted is that?"

Silently, I thank Carmen for her diary, which lays out the equal parts longing, equal parts hatred she feels for Tiffany Lazer and her snobby circle of friends. From what I can tell, everything between Carmen and Tiffany is some kind of weird contest for supremacy, though they seem to have nothing in common but the singing thing.

I notice a few of the other St. Joseph's girls hanging on every word Tiffany says, giving me the once-over while they're doing it. I feel a stab of pity for Carmen—why does she care so much about what the others think?

And they say girls don't like blood sports. My noncommittal "Oh?" is a little more antagonistic than I intended.

But Tiffany only hears what she wants to hear, and it's enough to prompt her to spill her guts about how Ryan Daley is *this far away* from being locked up in a mental institution for turning vigilante and stalking people he thinks might be responsible for his sister's abduction.

"She was taken right out of her bedroom," Tiffany says as Paradise High's music director, Mr. Masson, a tired-looking little man with wild hair and eyeglasses, taps the podium microphone with his stubby fingers. People wince at the vicious feedback he triggers, but they keep right on talking. Two spots of hectic color appear on his cheekbones.

"No signs of forced entry or anything," Tiffany continues airily.

Which would explain the invisible force field that seemed to surround Mr. Daley in the car park the other day. To most of the citizens of Paradise, it probably looks like an inside job. It also goes some way to explaining why Louisa Daley resembles a walking corpse and is on the brink of implosion, like a dying sun. Such a corrosive thing, doubt.

"Lauren was a soprano, just like we are," Tiffany adds. "Blond, incredibly bright, beautiful, too. The whole package." She looks me up and down as if to say, *Everything you're not, baby.*

I wonder again why Carmen wants this bitch to like her so badly.

"*Everyone* at Paradise High gives Ryan a wide berth," Tiffany says as Mr. Masson tries and fails to get our attention once again. "He's a weirdo loner with a hair-trigger temper and a *gun*. People have seen him pull one. They say there was blood *everywhere*."

The two statements are complete non sequiturs unless you draw an unsavory line between them.

Carmen wrinkles her brow, me doing it. "So people think Ryan might be in on it, too?" I say. "The father did it? Maybe the son? Both involved. Some weird psycho-sexual thing? Maybe the mother knows something?"

Tiffany nods enthusiastically. "Better watch your step. Sleep with one eye open."

She grins at the girl sitting on her other side, as if I'm not right there. *Like anyone would want to jump your bones.* It's clear to me what they're thinking.

"Well, thanks for the info," I reply coolly, staring down the other girl, who looks away uncomfortably. Bet Carmen's never given her the evil eye before. It feels good doing it. I stare down a few more of the others for good measure, and the St. Joseph's sopranos suddenly look everywhere but at me, their eyes scattering like startled birds.

"Consider it a community service." Tiffany laughs, oblivious to Carmen's odd steeliness or its weird effect on her posse. Well, she wouldn't notice anyway.

"And can you believe they roped in extra students from Little Falls and Port Marie for this musical 'soirée'?" she adds. "It's still going to sound like *shit*."

Mr. Masson makes us all jump by abruptly turning up the assembly hall's ancient sound system loud enough to split our heads open. The vast swell of a massive pipe organ is followed by the sounds of a giant prerecorded orchestra, and it's suddenly a mad, page-turning scramble to get to the opening bars of . . . uh, oh, yes, *Hymnus: Veni, creator spiritus.* Know it? I'm right with you. The score looks as unfathomable this morning as it did last night. And where does the choir come in again?

I glance sideways at Tiffany, and she's looking straight ahead at Mr. Masson, poised to sing. Always ready, always pulled together. Something Carmen wishes she was every minute of her waking life. People want funny things.

I follow Tiffany's flying finger to the point where her manicured nail leaves off the page and her voice takes over, and suddenly, my eyes narrow in shocked recognition. I have seen what I should have seen last night: Part One of Mahler's Symphony no. 8 is not in French, or German, or Italian. Languages that casually litter the margins of the score, with which I have little affinity, knowledge, or patience.

I should have focused on the title of the opening hymn.

Like the title, the hymn is in *Latin*. Untranslated Latin.

As the girls of St. Joseph's Chamber Choir begin to blow away the competition with their incredible singing, I realize that I understand every single word they are saying as if it is the language in which I think, in which I dream.

They sing:

Veni, creator spiritus
mentes tuorum visita

Come, Creator Spirit
visit the minds of your people

Creator Spirit. The words send a lick of lightning down my spine, the repeating crash of the organ causing little aftershocks in my system.

And the music? It's like there are *seraphim* in the room with us. Forget about the hair spray, the injudicious use of mascara, face bronzer, concealer, eyeshadow, pout-enhancing lip venom. Shut my eyes and I *could* be sitting among angels. The sound is tearing at my soul. It's so joyous, so sublime, so incredibly fast, loud, complex. Beautiful. If I'd ever heard this music before in my entire benighted existence, I'm sure I would have remembered it.

The girls of St. Joseph's have long since split into two distinct bodies of voices, two choirs—clear, bright, and pure—but, stunned by my new comprehension, I do not open my mouth or attempt to keep up. Neither does most of the room. A few brave souls do their own interesting jazz interpretations of Mahler beneath the main action, but these are largely lost in the maelstrom of organ, orchestra, and Tiffany, whose voice soars, higher, louder, purer than all of them. Heads are craning to get a look at the source.

"She's incredible!" someone shouts behind me.

I see the music teachers of four schools single out

Tiffany approvingly with their eyes as she preens a little and amps up the volume even more.

Poor Carmen. If this is some kind of contest, we are losing it together. I don't remember *how* to sing, or even if I can. Silently, I turn the pages with trembling fingers and wonder what else I've forgotten about myself.

Mr. Masson continues doggedly beating time, while the local girls telegraph clearly that we're all *dead meat*, and the boys place lively bets among themselves about which of us will get laid the fastest. I shrink down farther in my chair and keep turning the pages of my score a microsecond after Tiffany does.

The music changes as I listen intently. I hear bells, flutes, horns, falls of plucked strings. There is a quiet sense of urgency, of building.

"What's wrong?" mouths one of our teachers on the sidelines as Tiffany shoots me a surprised look before glancing sharply down at her own music then back at me.

A shaky tenor seated somewhere in the chilly hall launches into a quavery solo, and there is a smattering of laughter, like a reluctant studio audience being warmed up by the second-rate comedy guy. Moments later, Tiffany lifts her bell-like voice in counterpoint, and I marvel afresh. When she sings, she sounds the opposite of the way she usually comes across, and that has to be a good thing.

On opposite sides of our row, two St. Joseph's girls frown at me fiercely before hurriedly joining their voices to Tiffany's. Two more male voices wobble gamely into the fray. Together, they sing:

Imple superna gratia
quae tu creasti pectora.

Fill with grace from on high
the hearts which Thou didst create.

The words fill me with an abrupt sadness I cannot name. It is several pages before I realize that the gray-haired, hatchet-faced teacher from the bus, who is pacing the sidelines and waggling her fists furiously, is trying to catch my eye. People all over the room have begun to notice her jerky, spiderlike movements, and they crane their necks to look. Chatter begins to build below the surface of the incredible music.

"Carmen!" the woman roars suddenly over the music recording, unable to hold back her fury any longer.

I realize with horror that I have missed some kind of cue, and that it can't have been the first.

I shake my head at the woman—Miss Fellows, I think her name is—and raise my hands in confusion. She responds like a cartoon character, jumping up and down on the spot and tearing at her short gray hair so that it stands on end like the quills of some deadly animal.

Mr. Masson silences the prerecorded orchestra. "Is there a problem?" he says, with raised eyebrows.

The teachers from the other schools—a grim-faced, white-haired elderly man in a dusty black suit, and a lean, handsome young man who doesn't look old enough to be teaching yet—look my way interestedly. All the St. Joseph's girls are staring at me, too, and talking out of the sides of their mouths. It's nothing new for Carmen, I suppose. Others in the room point and whisper. *There she is, there's the problem.*

I am once more the still point at the center of a spinning world, and Carmen's face grows hot with sudden blood. I can't help that. I hate making mistakes.

"No, no problem," Miss Fellows barks. "Tiffany, you take Carmen's part. Rachel, step in for Tiffany. Carmen! Sit this one out for now. Take it from the top of Figure Seven."

Tiffany shoots me a look of immense satisfaction and takes flight after Mr. Masson reanimates the orchestra. Frantically reading left to right from Figure 7, I realize belatedly that Tiffany must be one of the soloists.

Shit, I think suddenly. *I suppose Carmen must be, too.*

The freakin' *lead* soloist. When she's at home.

CHAPTER
6

I sit there mutely for what feels like forever before the bell rings for first period and students stampede gratefully for the doors. The other St. Joseph's girls are borne away on a wave of male admirers, which has to be something new for most of them. Miss Fellows and the other St. Joseph's teacher, Miss Dustin, steam over in righteous convoy and prevent me from leaving, from even rising out of my chair.

"Not only did you embarrass yourself," spits Miss Fellows, without preamble, "but you completely ruined it for everyone else! Delia looks to you for cues, and what do you do?"

If Miss Fellows suddenly went up in a puff of

sulphurous smoke I'd hardly be surprised, but I'm only listening to her rant with half an ear. Something that Tiffany said before is bothering me, and I'm chasing it down the unreliable pathways of Carmen's brain. Hey, I have to work with what I've got.

Miss Dustin puts a steadying hand on Miss Fellows's arm and cuts her off midstream. I'm seeing classic Good Cop, Bad Cop 101 being played out right here. No prizes for working out who's who.

"Is anything . . . *the matter*, Carmen?" Miss Dustin says gravely from under her ridiculous bob. "You've been quite . . . *out of sorts* lately. I can *help*."

I have to stifle a burst of laughter that emerges as a fit of unconvincing coughing. From Carmen's point of view, there's not a lot that's going right at the moment, but it would be too hard to explain to Laurel and Hardy here. I shrug, when I probably should be cowering, which just sets Miss Fellows off again.

"You've been acting like a flake since we got here, Zappacosta. Tomorrow's your last chance, or Tiffany takes over, and you know where we're taking this piece, so consider it fair warning! Screw this up and you'll never sing a solo with this choir again. It will ruin your chances for performing-arts college, and I don't care how 'talented' people think you are. . . ." She lets that one drift, but the implication is clear enough.

For a moment, I feel a twinge of discomfort, like a pulled muscle. Carmen?

"Tiffany was always my first choice," Miss Fellows says sourly to her colleague, knowing full well I am still listening.

"Her voice doesn't have the brightness and tone of Carmen's, Fiona, and you know it," Miss Dustin murmurs in reply. "Carmen's not as mature a performer, but you have to admit she's really outstanding."

Miss Fellows snorts. "*If* she ever gets going! I shouldn't have let you talk me into it, Ellen. She didn't even try to sing. It's like she's had a personality bypass since we got here, and she didn't have that much to begin with. . . ."

There's that internal twitch again. *Don't worry, Carmen, I think I hate her, too.*

The music directors of the other schools file out behind Miss Dustin and Miss Fellows, talking quietly among themselves.

"Two weeks!" growls the old man in the black suit.

He shoots me an accusing look over his shoulder, as if the general lack of ability of the combined student bodies of Paradise, Port Marie, and Little Falls is somehow my personal fault.

"Less," replies Mr. Masson glumly. He doesn't look at me. I am just one more malfunction in a morning of malfunctions. "It's right on track to be a fiasco this time."

"Lauren Daley would have been able to sing that part," murmurs the good-looking, young male teacher, who seems to have forgotten that I'm there.

Mr. Masson nods. "A phenomenon. A once-in-a-lifetime voice. She could have carried them all single-handedly. People would have paid just to hear her sing, never mind the others. There's not a day goes by that I don't think of that girl."

What was it that Tiffany said again? It won't come clear.

"Lauren Daley is dead!" the elderly man exclaims, bringing my attention flying back to them.

All three reach the threshold of the hall. Somehow I can still hear them clearly, as if they are standing just beside me. Are the acoustics that good in here?

"You don't know that," Mr. Masson replies stoutly.

"Well, if she's not, she's as good as," the older man mutters as the group turns the corner, leaving me sitting alone in a sea of battered chairs.

What was it that Tiffany said? And it suddenly hits me in that dusty, echoing room. Lauren Daley was a soprano, a standout, a star. Like Tiffany thinks *she* is; like Carmen is supposed to be. That's what I was trying to remember all along.

I have to find Ryan Daley. If he hasn't made the connection already, someone has to tell him.

Maybe I've evolved, maybe I used to be some kind of impossible princess back when we first met, but Luc doesn't know me well enough now if he thinks I'll just sit around on my borrowed ass and do nothing. If you've got too much time on your hands, and you need it to fly, you've gotta keep busy. Rule *numero uno*, my friends. Worked out the hard way. Take it from me.

Ryan Daley had a reputation as a troublemaker, and I like troublemakers. Always have. Provided they don't hurt people who don't deserve to be hurt, I'm all for them.

But Ryan Daley refused to be found all that day. I went from class to class on the fringes of the St. Joseph's crowd, keeping a lookout for six feet five of total knockout, vigilante, gun-toting loner, and all I got was more gossip, conjecture, and fantasy.

"He's like the Phantom," snickered one of the gangly amateur tenors who'd hung around Tiffany like a bad smell. He was good looking in a wet, severe-side-part kind of way, if you didn't focus on the obvious crater marks on his cheeks from recurrent acne. "If it weren't for the Lauren thing, he'd have been kicked out ages ago."

"She was hot," added a towering, slightly over-weight bass called Tod. "Pity."

If he'd just come right out and said something tasteless like the world had enough ugly chicks in it without someone making off with one of the good ones, I wouldn't have been surprised. It was what he meant anyway. Like he'd ever had a chance with her.

"There was always something weird about those two," sniped a delicate, pretty redhead I recognized from a photo on Lauren's dresser. Both girls with their arms twined around each other's necks in a "Friends Forever"

photo frame. "It went way deeper than the twin thing.
They shoulda looked at him a lot harder than they
did."

"And you should know, Brenda," added the pimply
boy. "I mean, she's his ex and everything." He licked his
lips as he addressed this last remark to us, the interlopers
without the necessary backstory.

I zeroed in on Brenda for a second and wondered
what Ryan had seen in her. She was pretty, I supposed.
In a high-maintenance, high-fashion, don't-touch-me
kind of way.

Tiffany, Delia, and Co. exchanged satisfied glances
as the home crowd bore us toward the school cafeteria
for further updates on the Lauren Daley abduction
and subsequent fallout. All day, I listened quietly in
my guise as Carmen the screwup, Carmen the public
disgrace and nonentity, and quietly grew angrier as the
day progressed. Who says people don't speak ill of the
dead? Lauren deserved to be found just to shut these
phonies up.

When the last bell rang and I prepared to walk back
through town to the Daleys' residence, I was no nearer
to finding Ryan than I was his sister.

As I passed faded window displays that universally declared *Shop here for heavenly savings!*—every pun intended—it occurred to me that maybe, just this once, I really was supposed to sit on my hands and do nothing. The problem was nearly two years old, the girl had to be beyond salvation, and better minds than mine had already poured everything they had into it. Surely, the trail had to be cold. Only no one had managed to convince Ryan Daley of that.

I finally spot him crossing his street from the north end—coming from the opposite direction to me—toward his front gates, shouldering a heavy backpack. He frowns as soon as our eyes meet, and stops moving. I wave, which is a stupid, girly thing to do, but I'm no good at acting natural.

We begin converging warily toward each other again. But then the Dobermans start up with their weird howling.

By the time he and I meet up in front of the fence, they're growling and shaking as if they've developed advanced rabies, slobbering and clawing at me through the rails. Ryan's timing couldn't be more perfect. What would I do if he wasn't here to let me in? Scream for help from the street? Just *fly* over to the front door?

"Dogs don't like me," I say lamely, by way of a greeting.

"No kidding!" Ryan says incredulously, looking at my five feet of nothing and wondering how it's possible. "Just wait here."

Like his dad did on that first day, he hauls the dogs by force, one by one, behind the side fence and padlocks them in. The dogs don't let up for a second.

Ryan reshoulders his pack and heads for the front door without a word. Not exactly friendly. But he did call off the hounds from hell.

So I yell out loudly, "Hey, I'd like to help you. Find her, I mean."

And it's enough to make him look at me, really focus for a second. He frowns again, and I just want to take his face in my hands and smooth away the lines that shouldn't be there. They make him look older, careworn. Boys his age should be making out and getting falling down drunk, right?

"What makes you think you can help me?" he says quietly. There is no anger in his voice. Just an old despair.

I don't blame him for saying it. I mean, I come up to

somewhere just past his navel. As Carmen, I look kind of useless, even if I don't feel it, not on the inside. And all I'm going on is a hunch. Is it worth me feeding his delusion?

I don't like doing it, but I move closer and steel myself before touching his bare wrist tentatively. I need to know if there's anything in the rumors before I commit myself. Involvement is usually trouble, and, boy, I should know.

It begins as an ache in my left hand, building pressure behind my eyes. Then we flame into contact, but it isn't as if I'm being *immolated* exactly, burned alive, like when his parents laid their hands on me. Ryan's pain, his grief, is different because he believes Lauren's still alive somewhere. There's hope there, and it tempers everything so that I don't feel as if I'm standing at the heart of someone's raging funeral pyre. It's almost bearable. Like a dull ache; a pain present but contained.

I'm not really certain what I'm looking for, or exactly how this works. I get more images of Lauren, and I'm not sure if they're things I've seen for myself in her bedroom or that exist only inside her twin's head. But I feel it, too. There's something of *her* inside him that isn't just random memories. It feels fresh, almost recent. It's uncanny. Faint, like a graffiti writer's faded tag that refuses to be washed away by the rain. A reaching out. A cry for help. A faint *save me.*

The Latin comes to me unbidden: *salva me.*

I see fragments of the things Ryan's seen or done since Lauren's disappearance; an avalanche of scenes and faces and pure emotion. A lot of fear. Like today, as he warily combed a deserted complex of buildings on his own, jumping at shadows, testing the ground with an ice pick, when he should have been in class. Layers of long-buried thoughts become clear—memories of fist fights, confrontations, the inside of a jail cell . . . *the inside of a dark basement, with only the sound of someone's shattered breathing to illuminate the absolute darkness.*

I don't know how long we stand there, but Ryan finally breaks contact, shaking off my light touch angrily. The ghost world fades, replaced by the Daleys' front yard, the faint tang of salt in the air, the hysterical cries of the dogs. I am no longer deaf, dumb, and blind to these things.

"I don't need your pity. Or your 'help.'"

Ryan's voice is rough. He tries to open the front door

without looking at me again, prepared to shut me and an entire world of skeptics out if necessary. But what I say next draws his shocked gaze.

"I know where you went today, and I think you're on the wrong track. You should be looking at the house next door. If you're going to dig, dig there."

CHAPTER 7

"How did you know?" he demands in a low voice, pulling me through the front door and slamming it behind us.

He's still gripping the sleeve of the denim jacket I'm wearing, when his mother calls from the kitchen, "Ryan, is that you, honey? Carmen?"

Neither of us replies, each continuing to stare the other down.

Footsteps come closer and he suddenly explodes into motion, pushing me ahead of him up the stairs. "Yeah!" he finally shouts, from the upstairs landing, steering me away from Lauren's closed bedroom door toward his, the room on the other side of Lauren's bathroom.

"I was worried . . . the dogs . . ." Mrs. Daley says below us.

I get a faint glimpse of her standing in a doorway, eyes turned upward, trying to see what Ryan's up to, but he's a blur of motion. Always running away. Everyone in this house nursing their secrets, their wounds, in isolation.

Ryan yells, "Everything's fine, Mom. I have an overdue paper that needs work."

Then I'm standing in the dimness of his bedroom, heart thudding, close enough to him to smell earth and sweat on his skin.

It's almost monastic, the room. Just a bed, a chair, a desk, two blank wardrobe doors that tell me nothing about the person that lives here. There's no . . . stuff. Sports trophies, magazines, a stereo maybe, posters, smelly sneakers; things I would have expected in a guy's room. It's not so much a bedroom as a place to sleep, a kind of blank motel room tricked out in Louisa Daley's signature spotless monotone shades. Only, there's a giant picture of Lauren tacked above his bed, an impromptu shrine to his missing sister. She's laughing into the camera, head slightly cocked, looking straight at us.

I move closer to the portrait, study the wide mouth, the dark, lively eyes that are so like Ryan's. But she's a fine-boned ash blonde, where Ryan's hair is so dark it could almost be black. Physically, they couldn't look less like twins.

Maybe that girl was right. Maybe it did go deeper than the twin thing, and I should just extricate myself now, say it was all a horrible mistake, sorry for sticking my nose in, what was I thinking? But I don't. I like a challenge. Recognize it for a truth.

"She's beautiful," I say.

He lets go of my sleeve, throws down his backpack, deliberately ignores the comment.

"How did you know?" he demands again harshly. "About today. Don't bullshit me, choir girl."

"I saw you," I say. He doesn't need to know that it wasn't with my eyes. Trust doesn't need to come into this. "You were digging around."

His gaze slides sideways to his abandoned pack, back to me.

"Yeah?" He sneers. "You followed me, then. Did *she* put you up to this?" He rolls his eyes in the direction of the stairs outside. "You my new little watchdog now?

Got a crush on me, have you? That was quick work. You'll get over it; plenty have." The look on his face is ugly, self-mocking.

I meet his glare steadily. "It doesn't matter how I got there. But the church is too obvious. No one would be able to hide someone who looks like Lauren in the Paradise First Presbyterian Church and get away with it! Especially if she's some sort of live *trophy*. Think about how many people go in and out of that place in a week, use the church, the hall, the rec rooms, the outside storage areas you were sniffing around today."

Ryan's eyes are unfocused for a moment before snapping back to mine.

"Someone would hear something, see something," I say. "That place, that room you're looking for? I don't think it's inside the church grounds."

Ryan is so sunk in thought that he doesn't realize what I'm saying. I *know* he isn't looking for a body, but don't ask me how it works, this knowledge. He's looking for some kind of storeroom where a girl is being kept alive. *I heard her, too*, I almost tell him. *She was breathing. It was dark. It has something to do with the fact she can sing like an angel.*

"But I'm getting evangelical music," Ryan insists quietly, no longer looking at me. "Hymns, snatches of a sermon. It's *got* to be the church. It's the only one in town. Because, funnily enough—" There is no mirth in his voice. "The people of Paradise aren't huge churchgoers. Contrary to what everyone else says and thinks—even my own parents—Lauren is *not* dead, and she's close. Close enough that I can sometimes pick up her dreams and her thoughts—the stuff of nightmares, Carmen."

It's the first time he's said my name, and for a minute I'm not sure who he's talking to. Then I remember who I'm supposed to be, and I shake my head. "The rectory would be the better bet," I say quietly.

He looks at me blindly, his gaze still so inward-focused that he doesn't ask how it is that I know for sure that the living quarters of the church's minister are located outside the church grounds. But I *saw* the place he went to today, if only in illogical fragments. And there was no house there.

"You know, the preacher's private residence," I go on as his dark eyes finally settle once more on me. "It should be close to the church. That's how it usually works. It's likely to be less scrutinized, less frequented, but near enough to the church for you to hear the kinds of things you say you've heard."

I don't elaborate that I've heard them, too, through him, through his skin. Voices raised in vigorous Protestant song. An organ. Bible thumping. But the sound was too distant, too faint, not immediate. I perceived snatches of brilliant sunlight, too, falling slantwise down a flight of stairs, blinding when it came. One door. Two. More stairs. The feeling of one room flowing into another. A clock ticking. The sounds of cars leaving a nearby parking lot in convoy after service, horns tooting. Ordinary things. But then that feeling of terror. With light came misery. The light brought pain and shame and a feeling of wanting to die. I was sure—don't ask me how—that Lauren found the darkness almost more bearable than the light.

The sensation was fleeting, and to Ryan probably indistinguishable from his own nightmares. But in that strange way I have of seeing too much all at once, I saw it and I know that he is right. She is still alive and he still has some kind of faint, open connection to her. And he believes she's there, at that church. So, it's a starting point, of sorts. And it seems a good enough reason for me to be here, gives me something else to focus on other than myself. Self-pity wears you down, eventually, you know?

And admit it, niggles that small voice inside, *it gives you an excuse to spend more time with the guy.*

"Tonight," I say firmly, telling that inner voice to go to hell, "we go back after everyone's asleep, and we try the rectory."

Ryan looks like he's about to protest, but then his shoulders slump. "I can't understand why you'd believe me, why you'd want to help, when we're total strangers."

Not to me, I think. *There's something about you so familiar I feel the pull of it in my soul.*

"She is a soprano like I am," I say. "She is a singer. She should be with us. . . ."

There's no need to say any more, for Ryan's face is bleak, and he closes his eyes, swallows convulsively. Maybe he understands more, remembers more, of his night terrors than I give him credit for.

We promise to meet downstairs by the front door after his parents have gone to sleep.

I head back down the hallway to Lauren's room, shed Carmen's clothing like dead skin, and stand under the jets of the shower, head bowed. No thought, no action for a while, just sensation.

When I get out, there's one thing I have to do for Carmen. This is her gig, after all. And I'm trashing it. I need her to know that I'm looking out for her. I also need to know what my limits are, whether I have any limits.

Wrapped once again in a pristine white towel, I take a cracked CD case off the top of a pile of Carmen's things and slip it into Lauren's sound system.

When the music starts up, though I never feel sick and I never feel cold, I cannot stop shivering.

CHAPTER
8

It is past midnight, and I thought the Daleys would never go to bed. Finally, I hear them tossing and turning in their private hells, which is what sleep has become for them, I suppose.

On the stairs, I freeze momentarily when Mrs. Daley cries out, "Give her to me!" in a voice unlike her own. As if she is locked in a contest of wills with the Devil and the Devil is winning.

Ryan is already waiting near the front door, the loaded backpack at his feet, lumpy and misshapen. "Thought you weren't coming," he growls, hand on the lock.

"Wait!" I whisper. "The dogs."

"Oh, yeah," he says, frowning. "It'll wake them for sure. We'll have to go through the Charltons' place."

We head down the hallway back toward the kitchen, and Ryan stares hard at me for a moment as I cross into a patch of moonlight.

"What?" I say.

"Nothing." He shakes his head and opens the back door quietly. "Up and over. Quickly."

Ryan vaults the fence between the Daleys and the Charltons, who keep no dogs, catching me easily on the way down. Before anyone can see us go, we are already out onto the street and heading north.

"Church is this way," says Ryan curtly. I can see he's already regretting this. "Try to keep up."

He doesn't look back again as we cross block after block. Though the streetlights are dim, it's not hard for me to keep him in sight. The streets are deserted, the night chilly enough to keep even the most hardy indoors. There's nothing and no one to check our progress, and suddenly we're standing in front of a waist-high wire fence that separates the First Presbyterian Church of Paradise from the street.

In the dark, the church and its storage areas look

small and uninviting. We stand within the shadow of a huge spreading pine on the path outside the parking lot entrance, and listen for a moment. Like if we concentrate hard enough, we'll be able to hear Lauren just breathing, just holding on.

"Let's go," I say finally, giving Ryan a small shove in the kidneys. "Rectory is that way."

I point him toward a small, red brick, one-story house on the property next door to the parking lot with a PASTORAL CARE AVAILABLE sign stuck neatly into a garden bed in the front yard. There are no lights on. It's time to dig.

I walk forward stealthily in the absolute shadow of the tree, but Ryan doesn't move.

"Come on!" I hiss. "We don't have much time. Let's do this."

I don't relish Carmen's getting caught out here, in Ryan Daley's company, with no good explanation. I've got her into enough trouble already. Everything has to look like it's by the book from now on. I've made that promise to myself, and to her.

Ryan is still frozen in place, staring at me strangely. His eyes are huge in his face.

"What?" I say.

"You're, uh . . ." he says shakily.

"Spit it out," I snap. "Being a *choir girl*, I have a rehearsal to get to in the morning, and the night isn't getting any younger, buddy."

His hands sketch the air unsteadily. "You're, you're, uh . . . *glowing*."

I look down at my hand, hold it up to my face. He's right. In the absence of light, a faint sheen of illumination seems to seep up out of my skin, the lightest mother-of-pearl glow. It lights up the immediate area around me.

I frown, and then a hazy memory of the bookshop girl, the girl whose name I can no longer remember, breaks the surface of my mind. Her new boyfriend had said something similar once, on a walk home. It had been a moonless night. We'd been drinking and giggling all night long like thieves, though it had been more of an act on my part. I don't even like the taste of beer, but I'd downed a truckload of the stuff and it had still done nothing for me. "It must be love," I'd replied at the time, puzzled. "Or beer goggles, Bernie." He'd laughed and forgotten all about it in the harsh light of morning; and I'd left soon afterward, left the tentative courtship, the rest of her life, to her. The strange comment had completely slipped my mind. But now I saw it for myself.

For a moment, I'm grateful for the memory, it's a beautiful memory and I'll hold on to it for as long as I can. But I'm also angry. It's just another stupid complication for me to deal with. Right now, it's not supposed to be about me, although some day soon I hope it will be.

I let my glowing hand fall gently to my side.

"Oh, that," I say casually. "Well, I guess I won't be needing to borrow a flashlight from you, after all."

Perversely, as we approach the back door of the rectory and absolute silence is what the situation calls for, all Ryan wants to do is talk.

"How do you *do* that?" he hisses. "It wasn't my eyes playing tricks, then, back at home. It's really faint, but noticeable. Like you're *made* of it."

He runs a finger quickly down one of my arms and it's electric, his touch. I shake him off quickly, though a big part of me doesn't want to.

"Shut up and focus," I snap.

I scout the barren backyard for any signs of a

trapdoor, a basement; see nothing but withering lawn and concrete. These are not green-fingered people. Their concerns are clearly not of this earth. The house is low to the ground, ugly, and functional. There are no suspicious storage areas, no other structures at all. If there is any kind of hidden cavity or chamber to this place, it will have to be hewn into the ground itself and accessed from somewhere inside that house.

Ryan won't leave it alone. "Are you a ghost?" he demands. "You feel pretty real. Has Lauren 'crossed over,' is that it? Is she trying to tell me something? Is that why you're here?"

I put my hand on the unlatched screen door and say icily, "No, *no*, *no*, and *no*, as far as I'm aware. If I was a ghost with omniscient powers, you think I'd need to be breaking into some stranger's house with you? You think I'd even be here? I'd just walk through the walls, wouldn't I? I'm just a freak with freaky skin, okay?"

Out of ideas, I show him the unhealed eczema scars on both wrists, and he frowns.

"I'm not stupid," he growls, after a moment.

"And I'm not saying you are," I reply fiercely under my breath. "But I don't have all the answers, and that's the truth. Now either you start digging up the whole backyard like you tried to do around the church today, or we figure out whether this place has a basement from the inside. And I know which option I'm liking better, so get in there, hero boy. We don't have much time."

Ryan's mouth compresses into a straight line. I know we will be having this talk later. He pulls a pair of gloves from a side pocket of his pack, pushes me out of the way, and grabs the screen-door latch.

Of course, being Paradise, the back door is unlocked. Shooting me a hard look, Ryan removes a flashlight from his pack and opens the door silently.

We comb the house on sneakered feet, from room to room. Study the joints in the floorboards, lift up the rugs and bath mats, play the beam of the flashlight along the skirting that hugs the intersection between walls and floor, the single loft hatch in the bathroom ceiling; doing everything together, me watching his back, him watching mine.

The wind begins to build outside, rattling the windows of the little house, masking Ryan's careless stumble against the television in the front room, the squeak of the pantry door being opened, the sound the

cabinet door under the sink makes when it's pushed shut, of Ryan forcing aside the loft hatch above the toilet and playing his flashlight around the empty space above our heads. Nothing but dead air and insulation, his eyes tell me, disappointed, as he climbs back down.

The house gives away nothing more deadly than religious bric-a-brac and framed photos of the reverend and his good wife on holiday in the Sinai, the dust-gathering knickknackery of a God-fearing couple that is childless by His will. They sleep heavily, the sleep of the untroubled, and I am momentarily envious.

The only room we have not searched is the couple's own bedroom, and we stand outside the closed door now, debating with our eyes what to do.

What are the chances? I gesture. *She can't possibly be in there.*

I suddenly have a bad feeling about all of this. Something doesn't feel right, and I can't shake off the idea that Lauren's singing is somehow at the heart of everything and has to be looked at more closely. What we're doing here has *dead end* written all over it.

We have to know for sure, he signals back urgently. *You distract them, I'll search the room.*

I shake my head angrily, slice the air in front of me with one faintly glowing hand. *YOU distract them, I'LL search the room.*

He doesn't have my child's build, my quicksilver sight. It will be faster this way. In and out.

We stare each other down until he finally pads reluctantly along the hall and kneels in the broken moonlight streaming in from the long panel of glass beside the front door. I see him take a black ski mask from his backpack, then put it on, slide something else out of his pack, and slip it into his back pocket. Then he is outside with the pack on, closing the door softly behind him.

For want of a better plan, I duck behind the bathroom door across the hall from the sleeping couple and wait for Ryan to work his magic.

I hear the explosion before I see it.

four walls, four cross-stitched pillows, a dresser, and the bed. I look up. The ceiling is white on white from end to end. Seamless.

I need to get out of here. We were wrong. This is wrong. It has something to do with the fact that Lauren can *sing*. Again, I feel a twinge of discomfort. Carmen, trying to tell me something?

I am back at the door, my eye to the gap, when I see the woman hang up the telephone at the front of the house. I glance down the other way, down the hall back toward the kitchen, and see the back door begin to open, the leading edge of the reverend's receding hair line framed there. Things are about to get tricky. I forget to breathe.

My heart starts up a crazy pounding, blood in my ears, in my eyes. There's that twinge again, like I've pulled a muscle along my rib cage, like Carmen is trying to warn me things are going bad, bad, *bad*. What am I going to do?

The woman is closer to me, but her back is still turned. I have maybe five minutes before one of them returns to find me frozen here at the foot of their bed, like a person turned to stone, or salt. I have to move.

But where to? And how? Will I make it past the wife if I run? Or will she intercept me at the door, hold Carmen's slight frame easily until her husband gets there and the police arrive?

I can't be seen here. *I can't be seen here.* Carmen is in enough trouble.

Then something strange happens.

"Esther!" I hear the man shout loudly. "I need your help. In the kitchen, hurry."

The woman swings around, wide-eyed, and runs past my hiding place, down the passageway, responding blindly to the terrible fear in her husband's voice.

Before I know I am moving, I have sprinted up the hall in the opposite direction, toward the front door, have flung it wide open. For a moment, I look back and see the woman stop and turn in confusion, the man turn in surprise from the act of shutting and locking the kitchen door beyond her, holding a steel bat in one hand.

And I see it. He can't have spoken. He hasn't even seen me until now.

"What are you doing? Get her!" he roars, pointing beyond his disconcerted wife at me.

She blusters, "But you just said for me to—?"

And I slam the front door behind me in their shocked faces, dodging falling pieces of flaming pine as I run like I have never run before. Everything finally working together, as if Carmen and I have become a single organism at last.

I did that.

I did that.

Three blocks away, the knowledge takes the air out of my lungs, and I sit down hard on the edge of someone's driveway, legs trembling.

Behind me, a red glow lights up the distant skyline. The whole tree, as tall as a small apartment block, must be in flames now, and in the distance I can hear fire engines drawing closer. I need to make it back to Ryan's place before someone spots Carmen Zappacosta wandering the streets of Paradise with ashes in her curly hair. But I can't seem to move.

What else am I able to do? What else have I forgotten about myself?

It is only when I finally get to my feet that I see him. Standing across the road like a silent reproach, looking directly at me. He doesn't make a move in my direction.

Nothing about him indicates anger, or sorrow, or even interest. He just wants me to see him, to know he is there. Or maybe he has been there all along and only now have I begun to perceive him. His right hand rests upon the hilt of a sword, the blade of which is lost in his raiment of white. In his left palm is cupped a living flame.

And he could be brother to my *true* self, he could be my twin. I recognize the same features that greet me in the mirror. The same thick, straight, perfectly even brown hair, worn a little too long for fashion, the brown eyes. He is very tall. Pale. Classical looking. Broad-shouldered. Quite beautiful, taken all together. Like a living statue. Not Luc, but yet so like Luc in the way he holds himself, his bearing, his essential nature, that Luc, too, could be his brother.

What *are* they?

The thought rocks me suddenly with an impact like a small bomb.

What are *we*?

Ryan got it right when he tried to explain it earlier. Light seems to seep from the stranger's skin, as if he is made of it. As if he's some kind of being of pure fire. In robes so luminously white, I can't make out the detail. I look down at myself, and the illumination I shed into the chill night air is like a poor imitation, a mere shadow of the light cast by the burning man standing on the opposite curb.

I take a step toward him, pass a hand across my eyes—in apology? Supplication?

And, like that, he is gone.

CHAPTER
10

Ryan steps out of the shadows outside the Charltons' place. For a moment, I don't know who he is, because grief has made me punch-drunk.

I don't recall the walk back. I have rewound the faulty show reel that is my memory for any recollection of the gleaming youth who is like my male double. There is nothing there but darkness, and no one to ask, and the thought fills me with despair. I have never felt more alone. Suddenly I realize the value of what I might have lost, and it is legion.

Who am I? What am I capable of?

"What took you so long?" Ryan says, worriedly, lifting one hand toward me.

I bat him away. No more touching. That's just asking

for confusion and pain when what I need is clarity.

"You'll never get over that on your own," he warns as I weave toward the boundary fence that separates the Charltons' property from his home.

"Watch me," I reply thickly, and I catch the top of the post on the first leap and vault it easily. Grief has given me wings, the strength of Titans. I feel Ryan's astonishment behind me, more than see it.

He lets us silently into his parents' house, darting me sidelong glances. He trails me up the stairs into Lauren's room, wanting answers. Too numb to care, I watch him close the door gently behind us, drop his heavy backpack, and switch on the desk lamp. He turns to face me, arms crossed against his broad chest.

"What happened back there?" he asks. "You're like a different person, like something's . . . gone out."

That brings a hollow laugh to my lips. "You wouldn't believe me if I told you," I reply, groping for the edge of Lauren's bed, dropping down on it. "Where would I begin?"

Ryan frowns in confusion. "From where I left you, from when we were separated. Where else would you need to start?"

"Indeed," I say dully. "Where else?"

So I tell him what happened, except the part I don't understand myself. How, in my need, I was able to speak in that man's voice so convincingly, his wife unhesitatingly went to his aid, giving me space and time enough to flee.

I don't tell him, either, of my silent visitor, the shining one, the man of fire; Ryan and I, more similar than I first imagined. Someone missing all this time, someone lost. Like a phantom limb, the ache only now reestablishing itself. He wouldn't believe me. *I* don't believe me. It's as if some long-dormant part of me has begun to stir; so long imprisoned, it has forgotten the rudiments of language, history, feeling.

"So I did the right thing, then," Ryan says, relieved. "I wasn't sure. I didn't have time to think it through."

I look at him blankly.

"The tree," he reminds me. "I bought you enough time to search the bedroom then get out of there, remember?"

His version of events, so different from mine.

Hope in his voice. "Find anything?"

I shake my head, and his eyes go flat. He fumbles with his pack, brings out a . . . gun, waves it around. "Don't you want to know how I did it?"

There's that twinge again. Carmen. Can she see this? Understand what she's seeing? Is she frightened?

She would react differently, I suppose, but I'm too weary to pretend. It would take a lot to scare me these days. So I just watch him steadily as he points the thing at the wall and pulls the trigger a couple of times.

Click, click.

This must be the gun all the kids at school are talking about. It's big, black. Looks deadly. I don't think I've ever seen a gun before, let alone so close. Makes him look dangerous. Kind of . . . what's that word Carmen uses all the time in her diary? *Hot.*

"You shot the tree? And the tree caught fire?" I wrinkle my forehead, not seeing the connection.

Ryan gives me a strange look. "You think that's how it works? It's a flare gun. Add a bit of gas, and *boom.* Enough cover for you to get away. Got everything in here." He gestures at his pack, expecting gratitude, but, like I said, I don't do normal.

"So," I say slowly, "not only was today a monumental waste of time because you picked out the wrong search target, but you *wasted* a, what, two-hundred-year-old tree in order for me to make a getaway? I'd say the tree got a bum deal and we're all the poorer for it. I got myself out of there, like I always do. I can take care of myself. *You* bought me nothing."

Ryan's face darkens. "Yeah?" he sneers. "How?"

I'm lost for a minute. Should I tell him? It's new for me, this feeling of wanting to confide in somebody, to reach out. Though I couldn't have *created* a better person to want to reach out to.

It's as if I conjured him up out of my lonely subconscious. Though I must prefer blonds, mustn't I? Or rather, *the* blond to beat all blonds. But Ryan's still just about perfect for me. Every time I look at him, I wonder if he's real. There's the sense of the earth falling away at my feet, the dizzying precipice. I knew a man once, whose name I can no longer recall, who maybe had it nailed. He used to argue that what we perceive is wholly unreliable. How I railed against that. Because to someone like me, that's a one-way ticket to bedlam. All I perceive is all I have.

But I digress.

For me, wariness is second nature. I wouldn't know where to start with the whole trust thing. Best to go on as I mean to continue, right? Where would it all

lead, getting close to someone like Ryan only to wake one morning to find that I'm not in Kansas anymore? *Heartache and pain, begin again*, chants that little voice inside my head.

"Still trying to work that part out," I say finally, and he can tell from the strange expression on my face that it's the truth. He wants to know how I got out of that house under my own steam, I can tell. But he doesn't push it, he's a gentleman, and for that I'm grateful.

"I still think it's got something to do with Lauren being a singer, a soprano," I say stiffly.

Ryan's tone is dismissive. "You think I hadn't considered that already? Her choir stuff was a whole bunch of dead ends. I kept tabs on the people from Paradise High she mentioned spending time with. They were squeaky clean. All of them."

Not much I can say to that, so I don't. But it's important, and I don't think he's worked all the angles.

After a moment, he sighs. "What are we fighting about?"

"You call this fighting?" My tone is slightly derisive, but he doesn't rise to the bait.

"You still want to help?" he says tentatively.

I shrug. "If you think it will do any good."

His voice is quiet. "You don't know what it's like to have someone . . . believe you for a change."

He looks like he wants to say something else, but changes his mind, and looks away, then back at me. I almost reach out and touch him, think better of it. Sit on my hands for good measure.

"I'm tired; could I sleep now?" I say finally.

I don't really want him to leave. But we're going nowhere. And I need to do something.

"Sleep," he says with a fleeting smile. "You've earned it. We'll try a different tack tomorrow, okay?"

He shuts Lauren's bedroom door gently behind him.

I lie down on her bed fully clothed and turn my face to the wall. There's someone I need to talk to.

The hanging garden couldn't be more beautiful tonight. I smell neroli, jasmine, white magnolia, orange blossom, a thousand different blooms that no human hand could possibly have put together. It is an apology, of a kind, for the last time. He comes to me out of a living bower of flowers, a smile in his eyes, his hands curled loosely by his sides, no threat. Like a sun god when he walks. In robes of white so luminous, I can't make out the detail. As if to mock me.

I want nothing but an answer to my question. Which I am certain he already knows, has already read from my mind. Still I give it utterance. It *is* my dream, after all.

"Who is he?" I demand waspishly. "You're even dressed like he was; you don't usually wear white. It's not your best color. Don't lie."

In an instant, the garden vanishes and we stand in a flesh-rending hail of sand, at the heart of a devouring cyclone. Anyone else would be torn to shreds, but not we two. In sleep I am invincible, for I am under his protection. It is all for show, has ever been thus. I used to find it exhilarating, what he could do, what he was capable of. Now, I realize suddenly, it's getting a little bit tired.

"Look!" he screams into the teeth of the storm, throwing his arms wide, head back, displaying himself to best advantage. "I have remade the world for you."

"Don't change the subject," I snap.

The night garden rematerializes around us, new shoots breaking the soil at our feet, vines climbing, twining sinuously about our ankles. The fragrance of a thousand blossoms intensifies. Everything hyper-real, hyper-beautiful.

"Must we talk about him?" Luc sighs, winding his arms about me like the devouring plants. "I hate it when we fight. Our time together is so short."

He rests his chin on the crown of my head, and for a moment I close my eyes, the gesture so familiar I can almost feel it across a hundred human lifetimes. The bass note of my messed-up existence.

You wouldn't catch me saying this, but it's nice being held by someone who claims to know me better than I know myself, by someone whose entire, festering inner life does not become an open book to me at first touch. But I'm getting sidetracked by the moment.

"Who is he?" I repeat.

Luc pushes me away gently, considers me at arm's length.

"He is a portent, an omen," he says finally. "A dog of war. Heed my advice. *Do nothing*. Do nothing, and we shall be reunited in good time, sooner than you think. Act unwisely, and you risk certain destruction. I cannot be clearer than that, my love."

Understanding seizes me like a lightning strike.

"One of the Eight, then," I say in wonder.

Finally, They make themselves known.

"One of the Eight." Luc's face is grim. Light seems to bleed from him for an instant, then he is gone.

CHAPTER
11

The next morning, Mr. Masson tries a different tack, too, breaking the choir up into sections and assigning each group a different practice room, a different teacher. He calls it *workshopping*, but it's really meant to put a stop to the furtive speed-dating that is threatening to derail the concert.

The elderly, black-suited music director of Little Falls makes a move in our direction, but the lean, handsome, golden-haired young teacher from Port Marie's music program smoothly intervenes. "I'll take the sopranos today, Laurence," he says pleasantly. The older man stops, frowns, and introduces himself to the remaining group of female singers in the room, the altos. As they straggle out of the assembly hall behind him, they murder us with their eyes, every one.

"I'm Paul Stenborg." Our choirmaster smiles, teeth white and perfectly even. "Call me Paul. Sopranos, follow me, if you please."

Most get up with indecent haste, and file after him, chattering, into an adjoining building. There is a vague scuffle for the good seats. Near him, near the piano. By sheer force of will, the St. Joseph's girls come out on top. Tiffany makes sure she's front and center to the action, taking me with her.

The man is tall and Nordic-looking. Late twenties or early thirties, with ruffled sunlit hair and a bohemian edge to the way he dresses. Dark cords and scuffed workboots, artfully layered Henley shirts and a vintage vest hanging open beneath a battered single-breasted jacket, a thin, striped scarf. Steel-framed glasses, electric blue eyes, just a hint of stubble. Everything just so. A picture. Vain, then. I know I have come across his type before, somewhere.

All the girls sit up straighter in their chairs, eyes bright, color high. "This is more *like* it," Tiffany says with satisfaction.

Paul shoots her a quick look under his extravagant lashes, a lingering smile guaranteed to stop her breathing —I know, because I hear the catch, the reengagement— then he says brightly, "Let's take it from Figure One, shall we, soprani?"

He seats himself at the piano stool, begins to play with his beautiful, long-fingered hands. There is a flutter of movement as the front row—me in its midst— congratulates itself on its foresight.

As Paul runs the general chorus through their paces, I bide my time, learning the music, learning the faces, watching the clock, waiting—reluctant and on edge— for Figure 7. Just miming along, because I'm still not sure if what I have in mind is going to work.

It's stop and start. There are plenty of hands this morning as Paul patiently answers every stupid question the girls dream up just to get him to look at them. Like, "Ah, Paul, isn't that supposed to be a *demi*semiquaver?" ("No, it isn't, Mary-Ellen, but you've raised a good point there.")

For Tiffany, he has extra time and attention, asking her to demonstrate a bar here, a phrase there, over and over, with great charm and the flash of white teeth, until the other girls in the room are openly mutinous. But Tiffany laps it up, shooting me sly glances, playing with the ends of her sleek side ponytail, blowing us all away with her big, Italianate voice. Such a standout, such a talent, it's obvious what Paul thinks. He grins when he hears her putting the rest in the shade, his approval clear. There is electricity in the air between them.

We don't get to Figure 7, and I'm relieved. Maybe it won't be today.

When Paul finally says it's time to rejoin the rest of the choir, there are audible groans.

"God, I hope we get him again tomorrow," Tiffany says fervently. "What a total *honey*."

Then she gives me a piercing look. "You up to it?"

Everything a contest. I shrug. "I guess. Wait and see."

We file back into the main assembly hall and throw ourselves into our chairs. Mr. Masson exhorts us feverishly to "Take it from the top!"; the orchestra blares back into disembodied life; and the whole room rips into it. And though the basses are off, and the altos keep missing their entries, and the tenors can't keep the time, there's a growing sense that things may just come together. You can see the amazement in people's eyes.

It's beginning to sound kind of like . . . music.

All the smug St. Joseph's girls around me are poised like hawks for Figure 7. I'm packed in tight—Tiffany on one side, Delia on the other, girls at front and back—like there's been some secret directive to not let me escape, to block all the exits. Miss Fellows follows me with her dark eyes, ready to breathe fire at a single misstep, a single messed up demisemiquaver or whatever.

There is a moment of doubt, a tiny breath of uneasiness in me, a catch in my rib cage—*Carmen? Can we do this? We can do anything, right?*—as Mr. Masson looks straight at me, counts me in, drills the air in front of him with a closed fist so that I can't miss the entry point. Everyone is looking my way. And it's now, *now*.

And then I am singing the words I should have sung yesterday morning, the music I should have known yesterday morning, but committed wholly to memory in one desperate hour before Mrs. Daley called out that dinner would shortly be served.

The room bursts into open speculation, Mr. Masson beaming with pleasure—two sudden spots of high color appearing on his cheeks—Miss Dustin holding her chunky, ring-infested hands to her jowly face. For some kind of alchemy is taking place. It is Carmen's body doing all the work, her musculature, her impossibly tiny frame, her breathing, but I am the *animus*, the reason, the force. And I have remembered every word; sing every word as if it is a language that I alone have created. Together, we are sublime, I know it. Some things the body just remembers.

I see the dark-suited, old music teacher's undisguised excitement, Miss Fellows nodding tightly, Paul Stenborg's suddenly mesmerized expression, as everyone strains to hear my instinctive phrasing, my superlative attack, my entries, my exits, the clean, lyrical beauty in my voice. Not too big, not too showy, not Italianate. Something else altogether. Something almost otherworldly. Sweetness with power. The cadences rising and falling toward the ceiling, single notes hanging there, suspended, as if they have their own lives—are made of lambent crystal.

I'm leaving them all behind. They are singing, the other soloists—the girls of St. Joseph's, the quavery tenor, the hopeless bass, and so-so baritone—but they may as well be miming now. Tiffany is furious. Her face is lit up like a Christmas tree with ill will and irritation as she tries to outsing me, but fails. A lark striving to catch a burning phoenix arcing skyward. The whole room is listening so hard that the entire chorus, almost two hundred people, fails to come in after Figure 10, and I sing on alone for what feels like an eternity, and I wonder how much of this glorious sound is Carmen and how much of it, if any of it, is *me*.

Mr. Masson abruptly shuts off the sound system, and I stumble to a halt, my last word ringing in the air.

Creasti shimmers there. *Created.*

"Well, let's leave it there for now. We'll reconvene at four this afternoon," says Mr. Masson delightedly, eyes shining, as the room erupts into noise and movement. "We might have a concert on our hands, boys and girls, we just might. Good work, Carmen. Superb." He gives a nod in my direction.

Beside me, Tiffany lets loose a long breath, like a hiss.

"Beautiful," declares Miss Dustin, clapping me so hard between the shoulder blades with one of her man hands that I almost fall off my chair. "Really wonderful, Carmen. There was a quality in your voice today I don't think I've ever heard before."

I'm speechless, still grateful that my gamble has paid off. Turns out I have some kind of weird mnemonic memory for music and lyrics, and Carmen has a set of lungs to write home about. Who knew? It's a lucky break.

"You certainly showed us," Miss Fellows snipes nastily before moving away to speak with Mr. Masson, who keeps stealing glances at me as if I might dematerialize.

I think what Miss Fellows really means is *showed off*. I speak subliminal messaging better than most people.

Around me, Tiffany and some of the other girls stand up abruptly, clutching their scores to their chests like armor plate.

"I'm Laurence Barry," interrupts the elderly music director of Little Falls, moving forward with his right hand held out. Not scowling at me today, not at all. "Have you considered—"

Someone else cuts in before the old man can finish his sentence or touch me, which I'm grateful for. "Paul Stenborg," he says, as if he hadn't ignored me all morning, his light, luminous eyes looking over and past Carmen Zappacosta's nondescript head, her nondescript features. "Though of course you know that already. Certainly hiding your light under a bushel there, young woman. Extraordinary, so unexpected . . ."

I feel eyes on my back, and turn. Catch the back view of Tiffany tossing her side ponytail over her shoulder. She leads the other St. Joseph's girls away to first period without a word, and I know from the way she's holding herself that she thinks I've engineered all this deliberately to give myself a bigger profile.

Someone taps me on the shoulder. It's the tenor with bad skin who's been following Tiffany around like a whipped dog for the last few days. By the weirdly attentive look in his eyes, it seems he may now have switched his unnerving allegiance to me. Behind him stands the bulky, dark-haired bass singer, Tod, and three local girls, the witchy Brenda—Ryan's ex—among them, all watching me closely.

"That was *fan*tastic," the boy gushes, and I have to move back subtly or risk being engulfed by partially digested Spanish onion. "So are you coming tonight, or what?"

I feel Carmen's forehead wrinkle up, me doing it. If something's on tonight, Tiffany and her posse haven't bothered to keep me informed, which is typical, because

Carmen always finds out about the good stuff way after it's already happened.

"Uh, I . . ." I draw out the syllables hesitantly to give someone a chance to fill me in on the details.

"You *have* to come," purrs one of the girls standing beside Tod, a horsy-faced dirty blonde in tightly layered tops and even tighter jeans, with impossibly long and perfect peach-colored nails. "If only to put that Tiffany Lazer of yours in her place."

"She's getting on our . . . *nerves*," adds the other girl I don't know, a crop-haired, biker-chick brunette wearing way too much heavy navy eyeliner.

"Thinks she's better than all of us," the flame-haired Brenda interjects waspishly. "When clearly she's not."

"So, will you come?" Pimple Boy leans forward expectantly. I watch his Adam's apple slide up and down as I step back a fraction.

"Um, sure," I say, assuming a polite smile. "How do I get there, again?"

"Brenda will pick you up," replies Tod quickly. "Won't you, Bren?"

"Sure," says Brenda, with a sidelong look at the girls she's standing with. "It's not like I don't know the way to where you're staying." Her laughter is forced. "Eight thirty, then." She smiles in a way that doesn't reach her extraordinary violet eyes.

"Eight thirty," I agree, not sure what it is I've agreed to, but I'm no coward. Bring it on.

We leave the assembly hall in formation, all of them flanking me as if I am some kind of dangerous fugitive.

CHAPTER 12

It's eight thirty, and Ryan's escorting me out through the front gates after dinner, following the usual elaborate ritual of imprisoning the dogs behind the steel side gate so they don't rend me limb from limb like an ancient Roman sacrifice. He wrestles with the padlock and chain, and we're finally standing outside his house on the footpath.

All this time I've been conscious of his hand at my back. He's looking hot in a beat-up dark leather jacket, faded T-shirt, and lean indigo jeans. But I give good poker face, and he has no way of knowing what I'm thinking. Carmen's heart feels like it's just broken sub-nine seconds in the hundred-yard dash.

"You don't have to stay," I tell him tightly, looking up and down the street for Brenda's car.

"It doesn't bother me either way," Ryan drawls. "Stand under the streetlight, okay?"

We move under it just as Brenda pulls up driving a sleek hard-top convertible in an unmissable bright yellow. Her flashy transport clashes terribly with her hair, but it's not up to me to point that out. I realize suddenly that maybe Ryan's here to see her under climate-controlled conditions rather than keep me any kind of company. I'm not sure what to feel about that.

Brenda kills the engine, then looks coolly through her windshield at Ryan, who stares back equally intently from the curb. No one seems game to break eye contact first, and I'm trying hard not to laugh as the seconds tick by. I wonder how these two left things when they finally called it quits, what was said. From Brenda's expression, maybe what was *thrown*.

Finally, she slides her long, slim legs out of the driver's seat. She's wearing slinky black patterned tights, a barely there skirt in jewel green, and a purple cashmere pullover that goes unbelievably well with her huge violet eyes. Boho chandelier earrings brush the tops of her narrow shoulders. Her razor-cut, shoulder-length red hair is styled to within an inch of its life so that individual strands don't move in the chill night breeze. She's perfection.

"Well, look who's here," Brenda says icily. "It's been a while."

"Brenda Sorensen," Ryan replies through his teeth. There's a strange look on his face that might be regret.

Or maybe indigestion, the evil part of me whispers.

"Where *have* you been?" Brenda continues, barely acknowledging me, though it is me she is ostensibly here for. "You're like a ghost these days."

"You know what I've been up to," Ryan says warily, taking a step closer, out of the circle of light he's placed us in. "There's no point acting as if nothing's happened when I *know* she's out there somewhere. I mean, school's always going to be there. . . ."

And *she* won't. He doesn't have to say it. I can read it in his face. Since when did I get so good at doing that?

Together, they are a total contrast in height, color, personality. If Brenda has a nice, soft side, I've yet to see it. But she sure rocks her outfit and towering heels. Tonight, she's beautiful. One of those people for whom moonlight does wonders. I'm beginning to see the attraction she might have held for him. She's like a lethal wisp of steel beside him, crowned with fire. I can see how life with someone like Brenda would never be . . . boring.

"I don't mean to be *insensitive*," Brenda breathes finally, running the fingers of one hand lightly up Ryan's jacket front as if I'm not standing right there, "but Lauren would have *hated* seeing you this way. Running in circles. Going nowhere. I *miss* you. It might not seem that way, but I do." Her voice drops a notch. "There's nothing left to prove, you know." Her tone is almost pleading now, and something softens in the harsh lines of Ryan's face. "You've done everything you can. No one could have done more. She would have wanted you to get on with your life." Brenda's pale hand lingers a moment longer on the collar of Ryan's leather jacket before falling gracefully away.

"How would *you* know what Lauren would have wanted?" Ryan says bleakly.

"Because she was my best friend," Brenda replies softly. "And maybe now you're beginning to see that you're wasting your time when the people who are still alive *need* you." She steps even closer to him, her dainty profile tilted up toward his, earrings jangling softly. "We haven't won a game since you quit on us: the offense is a mess. And nothing's been right since we—"

"We've talked about this," Ryan sighs. "Speaking of circles."

Brenda leans in but then stops short, her attention suddenly arrested. She frowns. "Why are the dogs *barking* like that?"

Good pick-up, I think acidly. *Sorry to spoil your touching little reunion, but it sounds like an insane asylum to me, too, from where I'm standing.*

Ryan stiffens, recalled to my slight presence in the pool of light at his shoulder. "They're a little sensitive to—"

"The perfume I'm wearing," I chime in. "It's a doozy."

I'm about to move forward toward Brenda's car, fully aware of the fascinating situation between them now, when Ryan steps backward heavily onto my foot, pinning me in place.

"Hey," I growl, heart back under control and doing a steady eighty-two beats per minute. "I'm walking here."

"I'll drive," he says, his weight still keeping me in check.

Carmen's toes are beginning to throb, and I twist

my foot angrily, only to have Ryan stomp down harder.
Our eyes clash for a moment.

The look of delight on Brenda's face is unmistakable.
"You will?" she almost squeals, her violet eyes wide.
"Does that mean . . . ?"

"It means I feel like a bit of company tonight," Ryan
replies, swinging back around to face his ex-girlfriend,
his heel still firmly pinning me down. "It's been way, *way*
too long. You two wait right here. Don't move a muscle."

He releases Carmen's foot, and I flex it, feeling the
blood come rushing back.

"And I mean *wait*, pip-squeak," he hisses, for my
benefit alone. "You're no good—in the *dark*."

And suddenly I understand. All along, I thought his
attention was squarely focused on the fashion plate in
front of us when really he was on the lookout for me as
well. I'd be kind of touched if I wasn't such a hard-ass.

I glance down at my hands, touch my face self-
consciously, and wonder whether Brenda *sees*.

The dogs are still going mad as Ryan backs his rusting,
white four-wheel drive onto the road and slides out to
shut and chain the gates and let Brenda into the front

seat. She is a happy blur of accessories, coltish legs, and motion as she throws herself into the car without turning to see if I'm coming. As she slams the door shut, Ryan tilts his head toward the backseat behind Brenda's and snarls, "Keep your head down, whatever you do."

I nod tightly, still embarrassed that he seems to know me better than I know myself. We both get into the car, then slam the doors.

We set off through the dark, wide, unremarkable streets of Paradise, with its generous plots of land, its regular-looking two-car houses spaced at even intervals.

"I *so* can't wait to get out of here," Brenda mutters, her shining gaze fixed on Ryan's profile, like a blind woman whose sight has suddenly been restored. "It's a place where whales and old people come to die."

"Or urban refugees like my folks," Ryan murmurs, his eyes fixed on the darkened road ahead. "I wish we'd never come here, moved away from the city. Maybe it would never have happened. . . ."

As I watch through the thick, woolly bangs of Carmen's hair, Brenda pouts slightly and puts a hand on his arm. "But then we'd never have met, Ry! Lauren and I used to make plans all the time about how we were going to escape here right after school finished, and take you back with us, to the city. . . ."

"And now there's no escape for any of us," Ryan murmurs, and Brenda's fingers tighten briefly on him like claws. "So where *are* we going, Bren?"

"To Mulvany's," she says, swinging around suddenly to look at me.

I'm ready for her, though, and stare fixedly through the side window so that all she sees is the side of Carmen's head, our palely glowing profile shielded by a mass of dark hair.

I hear the slight jangle of Brenda's earrings as she turns back to Ryan, and feel more than see the curl of Ryan's lip as he exclaims, "That dive! Since when did 'the gang' start hanging out at Mulvany's?"

"Since Mr. Masson thought it would be a great idea to show the St. Joseph's girls and their teachers a 'good time' at Paradise's 'one and only international karaoke lounge.'" Brenda's tone is derisive. "It's so lame. Like all they'd ever want to do in this town is *sing*, right, Carmen?"

The word sends a thrill of apprehension down my spine. "Sing?" I mutter.

"Sure," Brenda purrs happily. "If Tiffany Lazer thinks she's going to hog the spotlight tonight, she's in for a shock. That's why I had to make sure you were coming, Carmen. You'll put her right back into her box. The music teachers all get hard-ons every time we have one of these interschool concerts," she adds, lip curling. "And when 'singers of the caliber of the young women of St. Joseph's are visiting'—to show us yokels a thing or two—the music teachers get positively *orgasmic*. Though it wouldn't be too much of a punishment getting into Paul Stenborg's pants. Everyone tries hard enough, and rumor has it that he doesn't always say *no*. He's always taking his little favorites out for 'coffee.'" Her voice is malicious, or maybe it's just envy, pure and simple.

What she's saying isn't really penetrating my consciousness, though. *Sing?*

I swallow hard as we pull into the crowded car park of Paradise's one and only international karaoke lounge.

"I can't do this," I say at Ryan's broad back as we leave our coats with the barely dressed coat-check girl and pay our cover charge of twelve dollars a head, unlimited soft drinks included.

As he turns to look at me, Brenda tugs hard at his hand and says brightly, "Come on, Ry! This may turn out to be fun, after all. "

We pass some seedy-looking, middle-aged regulars at the bar, who check Brenda out with more than a little interest, as we head toward a private function room in the back. It's decked out cheesily with colored helium balloons and two twirling disco balls that fleck the walls and ceiling with broken light. The space is dominated by a wall of video screens in front of which is a small, maroon velveteen–bedecked stage. Two of the kids from Paradise High are half turned toward the bank of televisions, crooning sickeningly at each other: *my . . . endless . . . love.* There is good-natured snickering and heckling from the tightly packed crowd of drink-clutching teens at their feet.

In the way that I sometimes have of seeing too much, too quickly, I pick out a tight knot of adults clustered across the room: Miss Fellows, Miss Dustin, Gerard Masson, and Laurence Barry among them, together with a few watchful parents whose eyes narrow collectively as they alight on Ryan Daley's tall figure. Other kids begin to point, stare, and murmur as they spot him, too.

Clearly, Ryan was never one of the choirboys.

Brenda practically drags him around the room on a victory lap. His eyes search for mine, and he throws me an apologetic look.

There must be almost a hundred people here. I zero in on Tiffany Lazer, surrounded by the St. Joseph's faithful, and Brenda's two henchwomen, Tod and Pimple Boy standing nearby. Pimple Boy hasn't yet seen me, and I duck my head down and push through in the opposite direction, happy to stand on my own.

The lights are so bright in here I don't need to worry about whether my skin's glowing. I clock that there's only one way in and one way out, and hope fiercely that, if no one sees me, I can hightail it out of here at the earliest opportunity. But I see another victim step up to the mike after a round of lazy applause greets the grating finale of the endless lovers, and I *know* I'm in trouble when a boy I don't recall meeting thrusts a drink and a plastic-covered song list into my hand and says, "Where *were* you? We were all waiting. You're almost up next. So choose, already."

I quickly chug the contents of my plastic cup, and the boy gives me a huge grin and two thumbs up. There's something in the Coke, I realize, because he's making a secretive *tippy-tippy* maneuver with his hand, his back to the adults across the room. Before I can say *no* to another, I've got a new cup in my hand, and he's standing there with expectant eyes, willing me to finish it.

"Right under their noses," he says with satisfaction, tapping the side of his nose. "I'm Bailey, by the way."

The taste of the spiked cola isn't unpleasant, and as I thumb through the sticky pages of the song list, I down three more drinks, thanks to sheer, fearful adrenaline. The guy's eyes are wide with wonder as he melts away to keep me supplied with more.

I look up sharply as Tiffany begins to sing. It's a song with a big, thumping chorus about survival and heartache, with a driving, insistent beat. It's a crowd pleaser with the girls in particular—they're all throwing their hands in the air and screaming along with the words, every single one of which they seem to have committed to memory. Of course, being me, I have no recollection of this song and remain unmoved in the heaving, thrusting bedlam.

Tiffany's *beat-that* stare reaches me over the heads of the throng as she continues to belt out the words, and that cold feeling in my spine returns, the sense of being balanced on razor wire over the shrieking abyss. Everything a freakin' contest.

"Man, you can put that shit away!" shouts Bailey admiringly as he watches me crush yet another empty plastic cup in my hand.

That gives me an idea, and a moment later, I let my eyes roll back in my head as I fall to the ground. Like a tree crashing to the forest floor.

CHAPTER 13

A girl nearby screams, "Oh—my—GOD!" as the boy Bailey shouts above me, "Shit, shit, *shit*! Someone help me here!"

I keep my eyes resolutely shut as a swirl of activity takes place over and around Carmen's prone body.

"How much did you give her to drink, Bails?" someone hisses.

Bailey's panicky whisper confirms I chugalugged eight bourbon-spiked Cokes in one sitting.

"She's probably in a freakin' *coma*," exclaims a girl nearby. "She'll need her stomach pumped out *for sure*."

Someone bends to check I have a pulse. A touch so brief, there isn't time for me to make a connection, and for that I am truly grateful. From the ambient smell of mothballs, however, I'm guessing it's Laurence Barry who has taken it upon himself to gather me into his arms, cradling my head and shoulders off the floor. I continue to play dead for safety.

As Bailey babbles to a concerned parent that he only gave me one or two soft drinks before I passed out—"I have no idea what's wrong with her, I swear to God"— I hear Ryan's voice as he forces his way through the onlookers and takes charge.

"I'll get her home, Mr. Barry," he says firmly.

"She needs to see a doctor," Laurence Barry insists stubbornly. He continues to hold my upper body off the floor as if I am made of sugar and spun glass. For a brief moment, his grip tightens and the side of my face is crushed into the felt underside of his dusty black lapel. I almost struggle and give the game away. I force myself to stay floppy and take shallow, labored breaths, though the smell of camphor laced with old-man body odor, coffee breath, and hair oil is intense.

"No, really," Ryan insists. "She's on serious medication for her, uh, bad skin condition. She's probably just had a mild reaction to something she's eaten or drunk. Nothing sleep won't fix. She warned my parents all about it before we left the house tonight. It's no biggie."

Though Ryan wins out, I can feel Laurence Barry's strange reluctance to let me go as I'm finally passed from one to the other. To kick up the believability a notch, I allow my head to loll backward, and Ryan hastily props it against one broad shoulder. The leather of his jacket is cold and supple, and I resist the urge to turn my face farther toward him and breathe in his addictive clean male smell.

Carmen's heart takes off again, and for a moment all I can hear is the pounding of her blood.

"She's just trying to spoil it for me!" I hear Tiffany snipe into the microphone, cut off mid-crescendo, mid-chorus. "She's always been a jealous little *bitch*. This is another *stunt*, I tell you."

"Hurry back, Ry!" Brenda wails. "Why does this always happen to *me*?"

As we stride through Mulvany's, leaving hubbub and consternation in our wake, Ryan whispers curiously into my closed eyelids, "Now, what was all that for, pipsqueak?"

"Put me down! *Ry*," I say as we hit the icy parking lot. I kick a little for emphasis.

"Not a chance," he answers good-humoredly. "One, because you've still got an audience—you've really managed to get on that Tiffany's nerves, haven't you?— and two, you don't weigh anything. I'm kind of enjoying your helpless maiden act. It makes a change from the usual cold front you put on."

He eases me into the passenger seat, and I freeze as a deep male voice I don't recognize says behind him, "How's your mother, Ryan? We don't see her out and about as much as we used to. Betty's been worried about her."

Ryan shuts the door firmly on me, and I slide down in the seat and face away from the window where a man is peering at my prone figure. I make sure I lie on my hands, and let my hair fall a little farther all over my face so that no part of my skin is clearly visible, the very picture of wayward teen drunkenness.

"She's fine, Mr. Collins," Ryan replies lightly, moving to block his view of me. The neon light advertising MULVANY'S-MULVANY'S-MULVANY'S in a constant, epilepsy-inducing staccato diminishes in the car's interior. "As much as can be expected anyway."

"No new developments?" continues the man earnestly. "You know, we've told your father over and over, if there's anything we can do to help . . ."

"Thanks, Mr. Collins," Ryan says, shaking the man's hand and moving around the car toward the driver's seat to end the conversation. I watch him through my slightly cranked-open eyelids. "You know how difficult Dad can be. . . ." He slides into the car and tips the man a wave.

I clearly pick up the man's reply, "Half his trouble . . ." as Ryan starts the car and begins to pull out of the car park.

When Mulvany's is a distant blur in the driver's mirror, I slide into a sitting position and push Carmen's hair out of her eyes, tuck it behind her ears, with faintly glimmering hands. Ryan shoots me a quick look, his expression quizzical, before it's eyes front again.

"You don't really need your stomach pumped out, do you?" he laughs. "Bailey seemed convinced you'd had eight bourbon and Cokes."

"I did," I reply.

Ryan whistles. "You sure?"

I nod. "But I'm fine."

"You shouldn't be." His eyes flick to me, then back to the road. "You really *should* be in a coma the way Bailey mixes his drinks. Approximately nine parts bourbon to one part Coke—if you were lucky."

Whatever that "bourbon" stuff was, it hardly signified. I felt it evaporate along Carmen's nerve endings like gas poured on a bonfire, quickly burned off. Leaving hardly an aftertaste.

"The drinks were pleasant but not unduly . . . troubling," I say, and shrug.

Ryan lets loose another uneasy laugh. "Why the fainting act, anyway? From what Tod and Clint were telling me back there, you would've blown Tiffany away. Why didn't you sing?"

So Pimple Boy's name is Clint. I wonder if he and Ryan used to be friends. Whether the three girls and three boys used to triple date, or whatever it is that small-town youth do around here.

"I don't know any popular music," I reply after a moment.

Which is true. I don't. Apart from the Mahler I've only recently committed to memory, I don't recall any music at all. Just another failing of my diseased mind.

Maybe something expurgated to keep me safe. Or off balance.

Ryan shoots me a disbelieving stare before refocusing on the road. "You're shitting me, right?"

"Nope," I say casually, as we pull up to the Daleys' chained front gates. "I guess I just like Mahler."

Ryan lets the engine idle for a moment, turns to face me. "You *are* unreal," he mutters. He pops his seat belt, then the door, and adds, not looking at me, "Sometimes . . . it's like you're two different people, you know?"

I watch as he enacts the usual ritual that entails getting into the Daleys' place these days—unlock the heavy padlock that anchors the chain, unwind the heavy chain that anchors the gates, open the gates, return to the car, drive it forward, then do it all over again, except in reverse. I can see what Stewart Daley was thinking when he came up with the new security measures, but that saying about horses having already bolted springs to mind. Neither the dogs nor the chains will bring Lauren back.

When the car finally stops, I open the front passenger door; the dogs catch my scent and whine, then begin snarling and howling in earnest. Barreling into the barred side gate repeatedly with their bullet-shaped heads and their hard, muscular bodies, as if they have temporarily lost their minds.

"Welcome home, honey," Ryan says, helping me down out of his car.

We head up the stairs toward Lauren's bedroom. Apart from a dim nightlight on the upstairs landing, the house is in darkness and very quiet. All the bedroom doors, each blank white and identical, are neatly closed, as they have been each time I've returned to this house from school. I imagine Mrs. Daley's silent figure daily cleaning, cleaning. Putting everything but the thing she most desires, most longs for, back in its proper place.

"You aren't too tired to, uh, talk?" Ryan asks as he follows me across the landing to Lauren's bedroom door.

I'm in no mood for questions, but part of me is glad to have his company. Too glad. It could get to be a habit, and the thought makes me sound surly as I snarl, "I'm rarely tired."

He takes that as the ungracious yes it's supposed to be. But it's true. I don't sleep very well. Still, it doesn't slow me down any.

mercy

I turn the doorknob with one faintly glowing hand. As the door swings wide and I turn on the light, I see— Mr. Daley standing in the middle of his daughter's bedroom, holding a short white nightgown that must have belonged to her against his cheek. He is crooning softly, the sound making goose flesh rise instantly across the surface of Carmen's skin.

126

CHAPTER
14

"Christ, Dad," Ryan hisses, darting a look down the hallway at his parents' closed bedroom door. "What are you *doing* here? Jesus."

Stewart Daley's eyes are open and there are traces of tears on his cheeks, but there's a slackness in his features that isn't ordinarily there. I wave one hand in front of his face as he continues to make that soft, awful sound, rocking slightly on the balls of his feet. I circle him a couple of times to make sure.

"He's not, uh, *here*," I murmur, after a moment.

"What do you mean?" Ryan says sharply.

He pulls the faded nightdress roughly out of his father's hands and throws it onto Lauren's bed, then gives him a hard shake. The two men, of a height, eye to unseeing eye.

Lauren's wardrobe door is open, its little automatic light on. I walk carefully around Ryan's father and pick up the nightie, throw it back inside untidily, close the door.

"He's . . ." What is the word I'm searching for? "Sleep . . . walking."

Ryan lets go of his father's shoulders as if electrified.

"I thought he'd got . . . over that," he says, after a long pause. "He hasn't done it for over a year. He did it a lot when Lauren was first . . . taken." There's that pause again, like he's measuring his words carefully. "Mom and I didn't really bring it up with him, and it stopped, after a while. And when he woke, he never remembered a thing."

"And that's what will happen tonight," I say quietly, taking the sleeping man carefully by the sleeve and turning him slowly around to face the hallway. He goes quiet and still, his eyes blank, dark pools.

Ryan hurries down the hall to his parents' room and I hear a flurry of quiet words. Mrs. Daley emerges, more skeletal than usual in her white waffle-weave dressing gown, her paper-white face free of its usual careful make-up, her dark hair slightly matted from restless sleep. She takes one of her husband's large hands in hers, and Ryan supports him on the other side as they walk him slowly back to his bedroom and sit him down on the edge of the bed.

Ryan's mother doesn't look at me all the while, and I withdraw back into Lauren's bedroom to reduce the woman's obvious distress. I see her gently close the master bedroom door until only a narrow sliver of off-white carpet is visible. The sound of voices never rises above a murmur.

Ryan joins me a moment later, turns Lauren's white desk chair around, and straddles it, facing me.

"He didn't do it," he says simply, his eyes holding mine. "You have to believe me. And neither did I—even Brenda will vouch for that, because we were together for most of the night. Still, half the town thinks it's an inside job, and the other half is willing to believe it. It's two years tomorrow, did you know? It's burned into my brain, how long she's been gone."

I am silent. I hadn't let Stewart Daley touch me for long enough the day I got here to make a judgment about his guilt or innocence. Hadn't let the maelstrom in his head fully play out before I cut the connection with him. Maybe he did it, maybe he didn't. I am sure about one thing, however. Ryan is innocent.

Two years tomorrow. Two years of hopeless leads, and suspicion upon this house. Where would you even begin to unearth a buried mystery of two years?

"Who saw her last?" I say suddenly. "Was anyone with her on the day she was taken?"

Ryan frowns. "She'd spent the day with her boyfriend, Richard Coates. But she was home alone that night because they'd argued about going to the twenty-first birthday party of some stoner friend of his. Lauren detested the guy. Richard and Lauren had *zero* in common, but they were absolutely crazy about each other. Though they had some spectacular fights. I could always tell after they'd had a bust-up, even though Lauren wouldn't say much about it. Mom and Dad were away for the night—at the theater. Mom always said we might have moved away from the city, but it didn't mean we had to 'live like savages' and give up on 'the finer things,' though Dad didn't see it that way. There hasn't been a play written that he can't sleep through from the moment the curtain goes up."

His mouth quirks up at the corners before his expression grows somber again. He meets my speculative gaze steadily. "My mother swears Dad was right beside her the whole night. And that's what they told the police. She still blames herself, you know. Hasn't been to the theater, to anything, since. It's like she cauterized that whole side of her brain," he adds, looking down. "The fun side. The ability to be happy. When we lost Lauren, we lost my mother, too."

He's silent so long I wonder if he is . . . *crying*?

"So, this Richard guy," I say. "He got an alibi, too?"

Ryan finally comes back from wherever he's been inside his head.

"At least thirty-five half drunk twenty-somethings insisted in writing that Richard was party hearty from seven thirty that night through till dawn. And Maury Charlton told the police he saw Lauren moving freely around her bedroom at nine fifteen p.m. *Alone*."

"I've got a choir rehearsal at eight a.m. tomorrow," I say carefully. "But I could always extend my free periods in the morning kind of indefinitely. . . ."

"You're on," Ryan says, a sharklike grin on his face, his understanding pitch perfect.

I should be in study hall, considering the population profile and proclivities of the citizens of Upper Angola or somewhere, but instead we're driving down the deserted coast road away from Paradise toward Port Marie. Along the way, we pass an abandoned military base, its mile upon mile of rusting steel fence culminating in a set of chained gates at least twenty feet high, peppered with the usual threatening messages about private property being exactly that.

A little farther along the stretch of swampy marshland that links the two coastal towns, there is a discreetly signed turn-off for an oil refinery. In the distance, I see a vast chimney, a plume of red fire issuing from its blunt concrete snout, hundreds of yards in the air. There's a heat shimmer in the atmosphere above the salt plains that run right up to the distant refinery gates. Apart from the flames, I see no signs of life.

"Nice place you've got here," I say.

"It's like the name implies." Ryan grins without humor. "Paradise on earth."

As we drive, he gives me a little background on the Paradise, Port Marie, and Little Falls triumvirate. "Paradise was a hard-living fishing port until that whole industry fell apart early last century, and people like my folks began moving in and gentrifying—you get the 'ocean views' and 'lifestyle' without the price tag, and it's only an hour and a half from the city. The old-school locals hate it. Hate us, I suppose. Port Marie's always been like Paradise's more genteel big sister—with better real estate and water views, less heavy pollution. Except for where we're headed, that is. Little Falls is exactly as the name implies: it's inland and features a small set of waterfalls that no one ever visits."

It's an overcast day and everything is gray on gray. Before we reach the obligatory WELCOME TO PORT MARIE signage, we turn off onto an unsealed road plagued by deep ruts and potholes filled with gravel and muddy water.

"It's like something out of *Deliverance*, huh?" Ryan mutters tightly.

I have no idea what he means, so I say nothing, just grip the handhold on the front passenger door a little harder so I don't look like I'm trying to throw myself at him.

A little later, we crunch to a stop outside an unfenced, double-story, concrete beach shack that never started off pretty and has been allowed to enter serious eyesore territory. Part of it was halfheartedly painted peach many, many moons ago, and the rest is well, concrete gray, with a flat tin roof and cheerless lace curtains at each of the windows. The front yard is scattered with the carcasses of slowly rusting machines, an overturned tin boat, and three outboard motors.

"Richard's into extreme biking," Ryan explains, popping the driver's door, then getting mine. "Lives with his old man; mother ran out on them years ago, so housekeeping isn't a major priority."

The contrast with Lauren's domestic circumstances is breathtaking. "Nothing white-on-white about this place," I say.

"You're beginning to get the picture," he replies, a little ruefully. "Come on. There aren't any dogs. Well, not that you can see anyway."

With that cryptic remark, we head up the gravel-strewn drive together.

"He left school last year, midway through," Ryan murmurs, as he presses the doorbell. "Now he just races motocross bikes, does the occasional exhibition or freestyle gig."

I raise my eyebrows, and he explains patiently, "You know, arena racing, aerial stunt work—real daredevil, shit-your-pants stuff. After Lauren vanished, he had even less reason to do anything else except occasionally go on the circuit. He's quite in demand, apparently." Ryan gives the doorbell another shove. "He's a freak. I don't know how he can live like this."

"He might say the same about you," I mutter.

The door swings open, and a sweaty, whiskery old guy, with more beard than I have ever seen in my life, peers out. He's wearing an open shirt, heavily stained under the armpits, and beat-up short shorts of an indeterminate color that show off way too much bare hairy leg for my liking. His distended, hairy, peek-a-boo midriff is unavoidably thrust into the space between us.

He snarls, "Don't want any. Gonna set the dogs on you if you don't get outta here, pronto."

Ryan gives me a look as if to say, *See?*

And I get it, and get that Ryan somehow gets it too, because there can be *no* dogs with me standing here, large as life, the stiff breeze carrying my scent into the house. The only sound I can remotely discern is the faint tick of a clock somewhere in the hallway. If there were ever any dogs, they must've gone the way of the machines in the front yard a long time ago, the lie outliving them.

"We're here to see Richard," Ryan says pleasantly into the beery miasma that surrounds the older man.

"Down at the shops," the guy says curtly. "Wait for him, if you like."

Then he shuts the door, hard, in our faces.

We wander through the graveyard of dead and dismembered motorbikes, mostly Japanese, some bearing fancy European tags I can barely pronounce. Forty minutes later, just as we're about to give up and turn back the way we came, a red two-door truck pulls up the drive, a mud-splattered bike anchored to its open cargo bed with cables. There is a slight delay, a detectable pause, before the driver jumps out and walks toward us, a young man with dark blond hair, shaved close to his skull at back and sides but forming a Mohawk at the top with a long fringe falling half over his face and his extraordinarily pale, ice blue eyes. He's in layered, motto-covered skater T-shirts—the sleeves pushed high up both arms to reveal forearms crawling with tatts—and cargo pants with more pockets than I can begin to count. Some of the pockets jangle and hang a little low, and I imagine more bike parts secreted in them, the boy half made of metal.

He is much smaller and slighter than I'd anticipated, and he looks very young to me, almost as young as Carmen does. Lauren and he would've made a cute couple, I decide. Like two dolls. A matched set. He couldn't look less like his old man, and I wonder if every day, the old guy hates the very sight of him because he resembles his runaway wife.

Richard's "Ryan Daley?" is surprisingly tentative for an allegedly freaky daredevil of shit-your-pants proportions.

"Rich," Ryan replies somberly, holding out his right hand.

The two young men—so different in every way—shake and hold firm for a moment, and I wonder whose grip is stronger. Neither looks away, and their grins are momentarily fixed and glassy. Unspoken guy-rituals are still mostly beyond my understanding, and I watch, fascinated.

"And this is?" Richard Coates says warily after they let go of each other almost simultaneously, like a secret signal has been imparted, both flexing their palms and fingers a little.

"Carmen Zappacosta," Ryan replies. "A friend of

Lauren's from way back, from when we lived in the city. We just wanted to talk."

Richard's brow furrows as he inputs my name. "Lauren never mentioned you, Carmen, but I'm always happy to talk. You sure, uh, chose the day, though."

"Didn't we?" Ryan murmurs, looking down momentarily before meeting Richard's eyes once more. "But Carmen kind of timed her visit to us for a reason. . . ."

I shoot a surprised glance at Ryan's profile, but it gives nothing away. Probably just a figure of speech. The guy's a good liar, convincing. *I* almost believe him.

He continues smoothly. "She just wanted to hear about Lauren from you. How you spent your last day together. It would kind of be, um, sort of . . . a closure . . . from Carmen's perspective. She's come a long way to hear what you have to say."

Again, I glance at him. He has *no* idea. Does he? I'm the one who's supposed to be preternaturally good at reading people.

Richard waves us toward a reclaimed park bench that's set up under a giant streetlight fixed into the middle of the yard on a concrete block. The light wouldn't look out of place in a park, or out in front of a government building. But it's evidently been placed here—with little regard for home decor—and jerry-rigged up with electrical wiring, so it can be turned on at night to allow Richard to work on his machines.

I sit down on the bench while the two men remain standing. Ryan's body language isn't exactly relaxed, and neither is Richard's, but they're not hostile either. Perhaps they'd be best described as watchful, because it's evident—even after all this time—that each still doesn't know what to make of the other. If Lauren hadn't brought them together, I'm not sure Richard and Ryan would have even been in the same orbit.

"We cut the last period of class that day to, um, hang out at Coronado Beach," Richard begins tentatively, his eyes briefly flicking away from the taller boy's.

"Near that turn-off to the refinery," Ryan interrupts for my benefit, his own dark eyes unreadable, "but the next crossroad down, heading in the opposite direction. It's not a popular hangout because there's a vicious reef just out past the shallows that gives the beach its name —the Crowned One. Plus, the rip's killed plenty over the years, and it's a little too far from town. It's probably polluted as well, given what goes on around there."

I nod. Nice and isolated, then. I notice Richard doesn't elaborate about what *hanging out* entails, and we don't ask.

"And then we had a stupid argument about Corey's party," Richard continues, looking down at his scuffed, old-school high-tops. "Things kind of snowballed. About my friends, what we were going to do with our lives, where we were going to be in a few years, and by the time I dropped her home—around five forty, the sun hadn't quite set yet, I remember—we weren't talking anymore. She just stormed off into the house, and I went and got wasted at Corey's with a bunch of friends, like I always did whenever Lauren and I argued, and by the morning . . . it was too late. To say anything. To change . . . anything."

There's a funny note in Richard's voice, like a rising sob quickly tamped down, and I look up from my seat on the bench and look away again when I see the wet sheen in the guy's eyes. Seems genuine enough.

Ryan's gaze meets mine. His look saying, *You believe it?*

It's hard to say. Though, being me, there *is* one

foolproof way to know for sure. A way Ryan neither knows about nor has any access to.

I steel myself, because, as I've indicated, what I'm about to do—when I touch someone—invites in the unwanted.

I look up into Richard Coates's face and raise Carmen's left hand reluctantly, taking hold of his wrist. It's surprisingly wiry and thin for someone capable of throwing himself and a quarter-ton machine through complicated loops and arcs in the air.

My left hand begins to burn with that strange phantom pain, and I feel that building pressure behind my eyes. The boy doesn't flinch, he doesn't even react, his features as impassive as I know Carmen's are. He just looks at where my fingers meet his skin, an unfathomable expression in his pale eyes as we flame into contact.

And I see . . . everything. Feel . . . everything. As he told it. And more.

Like what *hanging out* on Coronado Beach really meant to Lauren and Richard. The sun moving quickly across the sky toward the waterline, the waves racing in toward the land, as the hours pass through my mind's eye in a blur, the wind rising steadily, whipping harsh sand through her hair, his, as they touched, then talked, then began to fight in earnest, voices rising, body language hardening, growing ugly. The last hours they spent together played out for my benefit. The whole shoreline empty of life, as if the two of them were the only people in the world, the first two people in creation.

It's clear to me that although they hadn't seen eye to eye on about ten thousand things, they'd had a love so deep it was almost incendiary. Something truly enviable. Though Lauren wanted more from Richard than he was prepared to give. He could have let things continue the way they were forever, mainly because he—like me— doesn't do normal either.

There's a part of Richard Coates that isn't earthbound, and Lauren had refused to acknowledge it. I recognize it in him, because it's in me, too.

Ryan doesn't even know half the story.

When I finally let go of Richard's wrist—for all I know, it might have been a single heartbeat or an hour —all he does is tug the edge of his frayed cuff back over his tattooed arm. Unlike my contact with Ryan, or how I felt after his parents touched Carmen's bare skin— burned, excoriated, as if by acid—the connection with

Richard was somehow . . . different. He *felt* it, my mind in his, I'm sure of it. And it gives me pause.

We stare at each other momentarily before looking away from the incomprehensible.

While Richard's gaze is elsewhere, Ryan raises an eyebrow in my direction.

I think he's telling the truth, I mouth silently.

Ryan nods, a finality about it. I wonder why my opinion means so much to him, holds any weight at all.

After several attempts at polite conversation, Ryan and I drive away. I look back at Richard Coates, wandering his motorbike graveyard like a restless spirit, until he is lost to sight.

CHAPTER 15

"What happened to *you?*" says Brenda nastily when I return to Paradise High for the last period of the day, Math. "We've been trying to track you down for *hours.*"

Her two ever-present henchwomen take up unsmiling positions on either side of me, and I know they'll be personally escorting me to my seat today. After they work me over a little first. For a moment, I wonder if Brenda saw Ryan picking me up just past the school gates this morning, and wants to cause a scene just for the hell of it. But then I recall what went down at Mulvany's the night before.

"My meds reacted badly with the stuff Bailey slipped

into my drink," I say apologetically in a little-girl voice, hanging my head like I know Carmen would. "Ryan was soooo mad at me this morning. He was *dying* to get back to you last night and was pissed off at me big time when I finally came around."

The lie works wonders. The crop-haired brunette with the eyeliner and leather fetish, and the horsy-faced dirty blonde with the impeccable French manicure, fall back a step, and Brenda is practically snuggling up to my right side with a delighted "Really?"

"I so *told* you," insists the brunette from behind us. "It was obvious."

"Kayla had it pegged," agrees the blonde. "He's still into you in a *big* way."

"Shut up, Jackie," Brenda says impatiently. "What else did he say?"

We're right outside the classroom now, and I'm not even feeling guilty about what I say next, because this girl shouldn't be on my case. She's Ryan's unfinished business, not mine. He can deal with it.

"You really should hear it from him," I urge. "You two have *so* much to work out. All he can talk about is you. I'd give him a call. Today."

Brenda nods eagerly, while part of me grins inside. *Good luck.*

When I'd left him that morning, Ryan had muttered something about checking out one of Port Marie's only two churches, still fixated on his recent fragmented dream. I knew he would be pretty much incommunicado while it was still light.

"Just one more thing," I say, as we head toward a bunch of empty desks in the back of the class, away from where Tiffany, Delia, and the others are giving me snake eyes for cozying up to the locals and not making myself available for their collective wrath. "I'm curious, because I'm staying in Lauren's room and I'm virtually *surrounded* by photos, and I know you two were best friends . . ."

Brenda's "Yeah?" is slightly less chilly than usual.

"Was Lauren dating anyone when she disappeared?" I say, keeping my little-girl act going. "It's been bugging me which one was her boyfriend."

There are pictures of Lauren and Richard together, but no pictures of Brenda and Richard together, or Richard with anyone else I've met at Paradise High, so far, like Kayla, Jackie, Tod, Clint, or Bailey. Plus, there are pictures of Lauren with a couple of other guys I haven't seen around the halls. If Brenda truly was Lauren's best friend, I figure she'd have a handle on what Lauren's love life had really been like. Maybe it was a lot more complicated than Ryan realized.

Brenda, still wrapped up in thoughts of her ex, is almost friendly when she replies. "Lauren never went for clean-cut guys, only the freaks. She was dating a loser called Richard when she was taken, a real loser with even bigger loser-ass friends that I wouldn't be seen *dead* with; and before that, a geeky mountaineering guy called Seth, with a ponytail, who left town before she started seeing the motocross dwarf. Goes without saying I didn't hang with him either. A choir nerd from Port Marie tried to ask her out just before she disappeared, but she told him things between her and Richard were pretty serious—can you *believe* it?—and they couldn't be anything more than friends. Ask him if you like. He's doing this stupid Mahler concert with us. He's a 'soloist' just like you are."

She drawls the words *Mahler* and *soloist* as if they're synonyms for something filthy and unspeakable that could get you arrested. Anyone other than me would take issue with it. But I could care less, because she's just given me a lead that maybe Ryan has never followed up, never even known about.

The info about Seth the mountaineering geek correlates with the pictures I've seen jammed into the right-hand bottom corner of Lauren's mirror: of her with some incredibly tall and skinny outdoorsy type with a huge Adam's apple, bushy ponytail, reddish stubble, and a friendly expression. So I just need to look out for a round-faced, dark-haired, spectacle-wearing "choir nerd" who's singing one of the solos in the Mahler piece and who hails from Port Marie. Easy.

Maybe he can give us something more to work with. He might even *be* the something everyone has failed to see all this time.

"Well, thanks for satisfying my curiosity," I say mildly, as I slide into an empty seat by one of the windows. "You remember to call Ryan, now. I can tell you've got *a lot* to talk over."

Brenda smiles coyly as she cracks open her textbook. "Maybe you aren't such a waste of space, after all," she replies kindly.

There *is* a God, because at the after-school rehearsal for the Mahler concert, Mr. Masson tells all the soloists to sit away from their usual choir stations and away from each other.

"Sopranos and altos, spread yourselves out among your opposite number. Spencer, Jonathan, and Harley, do likewise among the boys."

There's outright laughter from most of the males in the room as three very different-looking boys stand up, red-faced, and fan out through the assembly hall, forcing their way past a sudden sea of extended legs, locked knees, and folded arms.

My eyes pick out the dark-haired boy from Lauren's photo right away. He's of middling height and turned out like a clothing-catalogue spread, from his side-parted hair and roundish glasses down to his neat navy blazer-and-polo-shirt combination; stone-colored, pleat-fronted chinos; and boat shoes. He looks like the kind of kid who gets his head flushed down the toilet at least once a day by rival forces, and Richard Coates's total opposite number. If Lauren went for freaks, this guy would have stood *no* chance.

I stand up as well, taking my place in the back row of the altos as close to the guy as it's possible to get, with a wall of snickering basses between us. A couple of girls make room for me with calculated indifference.

Tiffany Lazer is on the diagonally opposite side of the alto section from where I'm sitting, still simmering at her inability to get to me for the purposes of having it out over last night's case of *spotlightus interruptus*.

As Mr. Masson moves to turn on the ancient sound system that serves as our ersatz symphony orchestra, Paul Stenborg raises one languid, beautiful hand from the sidelines and calls out pleasantly, "Just to up the degree of difficulty, Gerard, let's have the soloists *stand* while the general chorus remains seated, hmmm? It will separate the, uh, ah, *sheep* from the lambs."

"What a splendid idea, Paul," Mr. Masson agrees brightly, clapping his hands as the seven of us rise with varying degrees of enthusiasm—four girls, three guys.

Tiffany, the only soloist still occupying a front-row seat, sweeps her shining helmet of blond hair back over her shoulders and grins in anticipation. Over her shoulder she shoots me a confident look that is designed to psych out the real Carmen. But I force Carmen to give her a brilliant, megawatt smile in return, lips drawn right back over the teeth, and Tiffany's expression curdles as she faces forward again.

Immediately, I let the lines of Carmen's face go slack.

Part of me hopes she'll keep up the pressure when I'm gone, but I have my doubts.

Ready when you are, bitch, I think, taking a deep breath.

The boy from Lauren's photo pushes up his glasses repeatedly and fiddles with the wristband of his watch, though neither needs any kind of adjusting. A nervous type, then, just like Carmen ordinarily would be. The other two boys are hardly any better, like a slapstick comedy duo with their obvious bobbing, shuffling, and gulping. All three are totally surrounded by the enemy as far as the eye can see, and are being given no quarter.

Delia and the second St. Joseph's alto, Marisol, nervously take their places among the sopranos, like skittish thoroughbreds at the starting gates. The orchestra surges back to life, the entire room lurching into Part 1 with the fervor of a sick cat.

As we hit Figure 7, and I soar into my traffic-stopping solo without a shred of Carmen's usual self-consciousness, I position myself so I can see the boy from Port Marie. I realize Lauren's mystery friend is the faltering tenor who always makes his wobbly, half-assed entry after mine and before Tiffany, Delia, and Marisol.

All of the soloists, apart from Tiffany and myself, who have no notes to sing for several more pages of score, have bumbled well into Figure 21 when Paul Stenborg claps his hands loudly and with evident displeasure. The whole circus shudders to a halt, and you'd think the other choirmasters would be annoyed at his high-handedness, but they aren't. It's a measure of the respect they have for the much younger man that they wait expectantly for his words. Even Miss Fellows looks attentive, almost deferential, and I wonder at it.

"*Infirma nostri corporis,*" Paul says in a ringing voice. "*Virtute firmans perpeti.*" The ancient Latin phrases roll off his tongue as if he were born to say them.

"Whatever," I hear the bass beside me snicker, hardly impressed. Though he should be, if he knew any better.

Paul's pale eyes zero in on my neighbor with laserlike intensity, and he turns his next wiseacre comment into a cough.

"I realize we are pleading with God to 'endow our weak flesh with perpetual strength,'" Paul continues bitingly. "But you don't have to be quite so, well, *weak* about it. And that goes doubly for you, Spencer." His voice is ferocious as he singles out the wonky tenor who flushes scarlet. "It's an *insult*."

And just like that, I have a name to put to the face. *Spencer*.

Spencer is still nuclear-threat-warning red as he pushes his spectacles back up his nose for the thousandth time, as if the familiar gesture will offer him some kind of physical protection from harm. A ripple of laughter moves outward through the hall at his expense.

"More *balls*, Spencer," adds Paul Stenborg in a soft but threatening voice. "If you please."

Spencer nods miserably. Some of the boys around him hoot with laughter and pretend to grab at the crotch of his pants.

"Ready, please, Mr. Music," Paul says, with only a trace of icy humor. Gerard Masson obediently flicks the switch.

Tiffany and I make a brief return cameo at Figure 20, then the whole thing falls into a heap again as soon as Delia, Marisol, and the boys realize they're on their own once more at Figure 21 without the two powerhouse broads leading the charge.

"Carmen?" Paul Stenborg addresses me suddenly with his golden voice and electric eyes, as if there is no one in the room besides the two of us. Everything seems to stop, even time itself. For a moment, I cannot look away from him.

"I know you've memorized the entire score from the way you're not even referring to your music," he continues warmly. There is an implicit smile in his rich voice, like sunshine. It suddenly occurs to me that he's a little like Luc that way, each of them possessing the same inherent, undeniable glamour. That ability to make others do what they want with barely any effort.

"Would you stand beside Spencer and sing his part with him?" he cajoles lightly. "It's clear you can handle a challenge. Rachel, is it? You can stand in for Carmen. We'll leave Tiffany where she is, no sense fixing something that isn't broken. That should work quite well."

I nod, wondering not for the first time what this man is doing here in this drab backwater, governing such unpromising charges.

Tiffany's brilliant smile dies, while a delighted Rachel—until now always the understudy, never the star—bounds to her feet. Now there are eight of us standing amid the seated and sprawled student host. Something about the setup tugs at my memory, won't come clear.

It's true that I have no further need of the music, though I wonder how Paul Stenborg could have noticed in the general bedlam. He would be even more surprised to know that I have the entire score, from general chorus alto to solo baritone, from timpani to string section, memorized now. The whole thing held in my head, able to be picked apart at will, attacked from any direction, any figure, any phrase, any individual bar or demisemiquaver you could care to name.

The basses between me and Spencer part like the Red Sea as I move to a position beside him. He is so hot and embarrassed that he can't bring himself to look at me, but I'm right where I want to be. I'm suddenly eager to get the singing over with and the guy to myself for a couple of minutes. It's approaching five, and we're almost out of time. I need to make my move before the boy vanishes back to wherever he came from.

"Good girl," Paul Stenborg says approvingly. "Shore the poor boy up. Play the Good Samaritan." He nods at

Gerard Masson standing patiently by the sound system. "Gerard will beat in the altos in his inimitable fashion, then away you go."

I realize as I tackle the tenor part—Spencer falling in a fraction of a second behind me—that it's way lower than Carmen would ordinarily sing. Though the notes trouble *me* not at all, I have to push through the strange knot in her throat, her body's residual reluctance to come to the party. For a second, there's a minor skirmish for control. But I always win, and so it goes on, our blended voice still pure, sublime, singular, and rare, cutting through the general murk and chaos around us, clearly discernible to everyone, and the cause of talk, talk, talk.

Several times, I catch Paul's remarkable eyes snapping from his score to me in fascinated approval. Gerard Masson doing the same thing from the podium, Carmen caught in a cross-current of open admiration. I know that if it wasn't for me, the girl would have faltered to a stop long ago under all the scrutiny. Even though Carmen wants to be a famous singer more than anything else in the world—I know, because she's written it in capital letters enough times in her diary—she doesn't really like people looking at her.

I may have plenty of problems, big ones, but that's never been one of them. The way I see it? You are what you are, so deal with it.

Only once does Paul Stenborg single out the boy beside me for further humiliation.

"Spencer, Spencer, Spencer!" he roars in exasperation as a passage of orchestral accompaniment begins. "Maybe you should leave the singing to the *genuine* talent and sit the next section out?"

Chatter ceases as all eyes fly to the young man still standing beside me, anticipation of a fresh kill scenting the air.

I can practically feel the heat coming off Spencer's skin as he hangs his head in reply.

But Gerard Masson has more patience than his Port Marie counterpart and will not be deterred, forcing us all, with patience and good humor, to attack the same stretch of music again and again until Spencer has no trouble with the pitch or the timing. There is a round of lazy applause when Mr. Masson stops the music at Figure 23, after the entire chorus and every soloist has made it through the section several times without mishap.

"That's a wrap!" he exclaims happily as people surge to their feet and begin leaving the assembly hall in noisy groups.

Tiffany storms out with her faithful entourage, without a backward glance at me or Rachel, who gives me an excited little wave, her bell-like head of sandy hair fanning out behind her as she races to catch up with the others. I almost want to tell her not to bother, because it's obvious Tiffany's never going to speak to her again.

Spencer turns to me with a relieved smile and murmurs, "Thanks. I just needed to hear how it sounded. Don't tell anyone, but I can't, uh, really read music all that well. And we don't have a piano at home."

"No problem." I smile back, and I'm surprised to realize that I mean it. It's gradually dawning on me that high school is like swimming with sharks for people like Carmen and Spencer. People who are born without shells, without sufficient armor with which to face life.

"Do you want to, um, grab a coffee?" I say, hoping my voice is hitting the right note of casual. I don't want him to get the wrong idea—and he looks like the type to jump swiftly to the wrong conclusion. I just need to talk to the guy.

Predictably, his eyes light up for an instant then go flat. "Mr., um, Stenborg will be expecting me to get back on the bus with the others. I'm supposed to be on the evening shuttle. He's my, um, music director. We don't have enough tenors at school for him to, uh, use anyone else." His tone is apologetic. "You should hear the others."

"You don't have to explain," I say quietly, my heart almost aching for him. "I'll go talk to Mr. Stenborg."

I head over to where Paul Stenborg is standing holding a clipboard, a cool messenger bag slung across today's arty ensemble of striped shirtsleeves, buttoned-up vest, slim-fitting dark trousers, and eight-up Doc Martens. He's like something out of the Prohibition era, a studiously tousled gangster. Spencer trails me uncertainly across the hall and stands some distance away, as if there exists some unspoken moratorium on him approaching his choir master any more closely.

"Paul?" I say brightly.

The man swings around, late afternoon sunshine glinting off his steel-framed glasses, his ruffled Nordic hair. His answering smile does it to me again, suspends time for a moment, the way Luc can, the totality of

159

the man really quite heart-stopping. It hits me again, somewhere in the region of the solar plexus, how beautiful he is. And how rare is such beauty.

I give myself a mental shake as he smiles and holds out a hand to me. Charmed by the gesture, I retain my wits enough to neglect to take it, and after a moment he lowers it back to his side.

"Carmen," he says good-naturedly, not discomfited in the least by my unwillingness to get any closer to him. "Thank you for being such a good sport. Spencer's always needed a little more . . . *encouragement* than most."

From the corner of my eye I see Spencer stare down at the floor, wounded, scuffing a semicircle with one double-knotted, well-tended boat shoe.

"But he *is* the best tenor we have at Port Marie High." Paul Stenborg's voice is apologetic as he stage whispers, "*Sadly.*" Not caring if Spencer can hear. He smiles broadly. "Now, what can I do for you? You passed our wicked little test with flying colors, I must say. Gerard and I were talking about you before the rehearsal began, and it was his idea to push you a little."

As if he can hear what Paul's saying, Gerard Masson looks up and catches my eye, giving me a conspiratorial wink and a thumbs-up from across the room.

Paul catches the gesture and smiles at his colleague before continuing smoothly, "Now we know for certain what a remarkable range you have. Ellen Dustin did intimate how truly special you are, but we really had no idea until this afternoon. You have a range of over three octaves, surely? With ease, I should say."

My answering smile is politely noncommittal, for who knows what Carmen is capable of without me? I can hardly separate the strands of us enough to reply definitively.

"Would it be okay if Spencer and I did a little extra, um, practice?" I improvise. "He just wants to consolidate some of the stuff we did today, and we can use one of the practice rooms here. My host family can always run him home later. . . ."

Paul Stenborg's face assumes an arrested expression, which changes almost immediately to one of open amusement. "That's very noble of you, my dear. But it won't do much good. Wiser heads than yours have tried and failed to improve him. Still, knock yourself out. You have my gratitude. And you'll have to tell me how you get on. . . ."

As Spencer and I leave the hall together, I can't help but look back at Paul, his back to us, standing there in a shaft of sunlight like something out of a living painting by Vermeer. He suddenly breaks the illusion of stillness by turning and openly meeting my gaze. Anyone else would have blushed at being caught staring. But this is me we're talking about, and I've always liked beautiful things. Know it for a truth.

I startle an answering look on the man's face of . . . admiration? It's hard to tell, because he looks away, and it's as if the room has gone dark just for a moment. Like the sun's gone behind a cloud.

CHAPTER
16

"I'm surprised he hasn't asked *you* out for a coffee yet,"
Spencer says glumly as we walk toward Paradise's main
drag, battling a headwind that, by all rights, should
knock Carmen off her size four feet.

"So he really does, uh, do that?" I say, intrigued to
hear the same scuttlebutt twice.

The streets littered with broken hearts. I think it, but
I don't say it.

"Yeah," Spencer replies through gritted teeth as we
stumble through the swing doors of a faded, nautically
themed joint called Decades Café. It's deserted save
for a lone, heavy-set female staffer perched behind the
counter, devouring a lurid celebrity mag. She barely
looks up as we walk by.

"He's always going on and on about 'genuine talent' and how *rare* it is. How it has to be nurtured, *like a flower.*" Spencer's voice is bitter as he recounts his choirmaster's words. "But I wouldn't know, because he's never asked *me* to go for a coffee, and isn't likely to. A, because I'm a guy, and B, because I'm just a no-talent filler. He's made that pretty plain all the way along."

We swing into an empty booth in the back, me facing the door, back to the wall. I don't know why; it's automatic, like breathing. The waitress throws down her reading material to take our order after a longer than polite interval. I order what Spencer's having, because I don't remember how I take my coffee, or even if I like coffee. I just know that people drink it a lot and that at some time, in some life, I must have tried it. The woman grunts something unintelligible at us in reply before stumping away.

"You know he used to teach at some big-name school before he came here?" Spencer continues, his face and voice thawing a little as our coffee arrives. Two steaming cups of oily black stuff that he proceeds to spoon three sugars into. When he's done with the sugar bowl, I do the exact same, struggling not to screw up my face when

I take a sip. It's like industrial-strength floor cleaner, except sweet. Spencer inhales the steam and hugs the cup gratefully with both palms.

"Oh, yeah?" I say, stirring again to have something to do with my hands. "I wouldn't know."

"You should," he replies with surprise. "You're really talented. One of those 'genuine talents' he's always going on about. He's really connected, or at least that's what I've heard."

"So what's he doing here, then?" I query as I pretend to ingest more coffee, wincing a moment later when I realize how blunt that sounds. Tact isn't one of my strong points. You've probably gathered that.

Spencer gives a no-hard-feelings laugh. "The official story? He'd had it with the snobby stage mothers that send their daughters to that place. Too much angst, too much red tape, too much flirting from rich, middle-aged matrons who should know better. Preferred the simple life—if you believe that."

I don't, and curiosity makes me ask, "And the unofficial story?"

"He *had* to leave because some student had fallen in love with him and was making his life hell. She was stalking him or something. A couple of *thousand* dirty text messages, almost that many physical confrontations, a restraining order later, and he'd had enough. She even lay in wait for him in his bedroom once, did you know that? Climbed in a window or something. He had to get the police to remove her from his home. It didn't stop, so he left the school, left town. Moved as far away from her as he could possibly get. People fall in love with him all the time. And I'm not just talking the girls, either. Don't see the attraction personally." Spencer shoots me a crooked smile across the rim of his cup.

As interesting as Paul Stenborg is—like an exotic flower in the arid wilderness of Paradise and its surroundings—I'm here to test Spencer about Lauren. I'm eager to see what he knows, but I have to go carefully or risk spooking him, and this is one guy who's easily spooked.

"Hey, you know who I'm staying with?" I say gently, striving for casual. I tilt the surface of my coffee this way and that, as if it has the power to tell me the future.

Spencer looks up from the table. "No, who?"

"The Daleys," I murmur, darting him a glance from under my eyelashes.

Spencer immediately goes pale and takes a big gulp

of his still-searing drink. He gasps a little as he wipes at the corner of his mouth and his tearing eyes with the back of one hand.

"Ryan said to say *hey*."

It's a gamble. I don't know if Ryan knows Spencer from a can of worms, or vice versa.

"Tell him, *hey* back," Spencer replies slowly, his eyes suddenly glued to the dark surface of his coffee. "They're a really great family. So close. One of those storybook families that you wish you had. *Were* a great family," he corrects hastily. "I haven't had much to do with them since . . . well, you know."

We sit in silence. Spencer fiddles with his watchband, looking devastated, then picks up his spoon and stirs his coffee again, just before he pushes his glasses back up his nose. The amount of tension he's radiating would make anyone think he'd disposed of Lauren himself. Maybe I'm onto something here.

"They don't really talk about her much," I continue quietly. "All I know is that they kept her room exactly the way she left it, and there's a couple of photos of you and Lauren still stuck to her dresser. She really liked you. Ryan said so."

That's a gamble too. But I know I'm on the right

track when he glances at me briefly before looking back down at his coffee with a strained expression, then shifts it precisely two inches left, one inch right. He quickly removes something imaginary from the corner of one eye, and I look away for a second, pretending I don't see the glimmer there.

"She was really, really nice," he murmurs, fiddling with his watchband again. "Patient, you know? And kind, even though she was one of those people that doesn't need to be. I really liked her. We spent a lot of time together doing the last big inter-school concert before she, uh, disappeared. Me being one of the only, uh, semi-functioning tenors from Port Marie, you see." He swallows convulsively, fresh pain still evident in his voice. "St. Joseph's didn't send anyone that year, so you probably wouldn't remember it. But it was a big, big deal around here. You know I was one of the last people to see her alive?"

I watch with interest as he swallows again, wipes a nonexistent speck off one lens of his glasses, and shoves them back on so hard that the nose pads push into the corners of his eyes, making them water some more.

"I can tell she was nice," I say carefully. "She had a lot of friends, you can see from all the photos. There are dozens. I didn't know you could have so many friends. I certainly don't."

Ain't that the truth, says that little voice wryly.

Spencer's voice, when he finds it, is windy, bereft. "We just *got* each other, you know? She listened all the times I needed to vent—and there were plenty. I mean, he treats me like *shit* in front of everyone—it's practically a school tradition these days, you know, the public baiting of Spencer Grady, because if the teachers do it, it must be all right—and I listened when she needed to get something off her chest."

"Oh, really?" I say casually, casting Carmen's eyes downward so that he won't see the sudden hot gleam in them. "About what? Was she upset about something before she, uh, vanished?"

"More like *someone*," Spencer replies, with a faraway look on his face.

I want to leap into the gap he's created so badly I have to bite my tongue to stop any words forming. But somehow I bide my time, taking another small sip of my unpalatable drink, dumping more sugar into it, stirring vigorously. As suddenly full of nervous tics as Spencer is.

Come on, come on.

I'm almost afraid he's not going to say any more, when he blurts out suddenly, "Mr. Masson was trying to convince her to turn professional. Forcing her, more like. It wasn't something she really wanted to do. She wasn't sure if that was the direction she wanted to go in. He was putting real pressure on her to leave Paradise High and go for an opera scholarship with a prestigious performing arts school; next stop, the Met Opera House or something like that. The extra coaching sessions he'd arranged for her before the inter-school concert were really wearing her down—before school, after school, lunchtimes, during free periods. And it confused things with her, uh, boyfriend, Richard, she said. She felt like she was being pulled in too many directions at once, and she wasn't even sure if she loved singing enough to make the kind of commitment Mr. Masson wanted from her. He kept saying he'd make her a *star*."

Though Carmen's outward expression is unreadable, *I'm* electrified by what I'm hearing. Mr. Masson? That tired-looking, shortsighted little man with the wild hair and stubby fingers, who cares way too much about adhering strictly to the tempo? Is Ryan aware of any of this?

"The concert that year was Mr. Masson's pet

170

project," Spencer adds helpfully as he drains the last of his coffee, licking his lips as they meet the sugar hit from the bottom of the cup. "It really mattered to him— he personally chose every piece. Lauren was like his— what's that word?—protégé." The boy paints imaginary quote marks in the air.

"He had her doing everything from operatic arias to Andrew Lloyd Webber, and kept telling everyone that she had what it took to go all the way to the opera houses of North America, Milan, Austria. The music A-league. It was like he was obsessed."

I discreetly push my coffee cup to the side, and Spencer, being sensitive to giving insult to anyone, immediately does the same.

"We should do this again," he says hopefully. "It's been really nice."

I realize that *really nice* is his default position; it's how he wishes the world, and everything in it, to be. And something close to tenderness wells up again in my borrowed heart. As much as I do *tender*, anyway.

"Yeah, it has," I agree neutrally as I steel myself and touch his bare wrist where it rests across from me on the table.

Just a brief hold, a moment of light pressure, but it's enough to bring out a cold sweat on Carmen's forehead as I flame into contact with him, feel that building pressure behind the eyes, search quickly for impressions of Lauren in his mind. The burning sensation in my left hand snakes rapidly up my forearm like a living thing.

Mercifully, it burns out as soon as I let go. Everything confirmed. Brenda was right: Spencer had been sweet on Lauren and was crushed like a leaf twice over when she'd turned him down, then promptly disappeared.

Unlike Richard Coates, Spencer has barely registered my brief touch.

"I was going to walk home. . . ." I trail off, hoping he won't insist on keeping me company, even though it's getting dark out. Or, worse still, insist on that lift I lied about. "Are you okay getting back to Port Marie?"

"I'll get Dad to pick me up," he says, a dull note creeping back into his voice. "Don't sweat it. Maybe I'll see you around?"

I stamp down hard on my evil inner voice even as I force Carmen to reply cheerfully, "First thing tomorrow morning, right? Maybe they'll even let us sit together again. What are the chances? It's been way fun."

An answering grin lights Spencer's usually solemn features.

I leave the café waving inanely, still no good at doing normal. As I watch him wave enthusiastically back from behind the window, I *know* I've changed in some way I can't quite yet define. Because in the past, I would have eaten guys like Spencer alive with no regard for hurt feelings, and laughed as I spat out their bones.

Night has begun to mantle the streets of Paradise. I hurry away from the Decades Café, keeping as much as possible to the bright arcs mapped out by the streetlights, although there is barely anyone about. The wind is blowing so hard now that no one's likely to make eye contact with me anyway, without getting a face full of desiccated leaf debris.

When I reach the outskirts of the Daleys' property, I pull out Carmen's tacky pink mobile phone and speed dial Ryan's number. Maybe I only imagine that her fingers are shaking a little.

"Help," I say softly when he picks up. "I'm outside the house and hoping you're in there, or I'm in big trouble."

"Stay right where you are," he says in his deep, familiar voice that always sets off that strange longing in me for some kind of normalcy, safe harbor, however fleeting. "I'll come get you."

The wind shifts, carrying the scent of me to Stewart Daley's dogs. Their sudden, unbridled rage seems almost welcoming, as Ryan ushers me quickly into the warmth of his parents' house, every downstairs lamp lit as if to welcome me back from a long journey. The Prodigal Whatever-I-Am.

"Mom's upstairs, and Dad's been held up at work," Ryan explains as he shuts the front door against the howling world outside.

He looks so good to me that I have to struggle to keep my tone light. "Enough time to catch you up on what I learned today?"

I head down the hall, shrugging out of Carmen's gray hoodie as I go, knowing he'll follow. I hug the knowledge to myself, before logic kicks in. I mean, the guy'll follow anyone to the ends of the earth if it means he might learn something new about his sister's whereabouts. Besides, Carmen's no beauty, and I can be a little . . . difficult. I admit it. So who am I kidding?

"For you, sweetheart?" Ryan grins at me crookedly —I know because I dart him a quick look from under Carmen's surprisingly long lashes. "There's always time."

Maybe I'm just imagining Carmen's heart skipping a beat.

You hearing this? I tell her, wanting some kind of affirmation that I'm not overreacting to something that isn't there. Of course, there's no reply. There never is.

As we come up on the landing, I glance down the hallway and see Mrs. Daley's wraithlike shadow moving against the brilliant white lamplight in her bedroom.

Wordlessly, Ryan and I enter Lauren's room together. He turns on every light he can find, as if to ward off evil spirits, before shutting the door. I place Carmen's hoodie down on the bed, walk over to Lauren's desk, and dump Carmen's satchel on top of it.

"The night she was taken was like this," Ryan says almost ruefully, propping himself up against Lauren's dresser. "Almost blowing a gale by ten p.m.; fifty miles per hour—at least—out on the water. No one would have heard a thing. When it gets like this now, Mom insists on lighting up the entire place. Dad and I do it automatically these days. We used to try to talk her out of it, but she's almost got us believing it, too."

Understanding dawns on me. "It's so that Lauren will be able to find her way home in the dark," I say softly.

"Something like that." Ryan shrugs. "Like that makes any kind of sense. Hit any dead ends today? I sure did."

I listen impatiently as he tells me about his fruitless search of the Port Marie Evangelical Church, before I lay out eagerly what I learned from Spencer. When nothing in Ryan's face changes, I know he knows it all already, and I'm hit so hard by a wave of disappointment, I have to sit down on the edge of Lauren's bed.

That's what you get for trying to impress the boy, I think bitterly.

"I remember checking Masson out," Ryan says. "He's got a wife and two small boys, one with some kind of learning disorder. They live out by the burned-down old cannery near the waterfront, and their place is tiny. It's not a church either. Like I told you, I checked out the Paradise High choir crowd and they came up clean. We could look at Masson again," he finishes doubtfully, "but it'd probably be a waste of time."

"Oh," I say, because there's nothing else *to* say.

There's a sharp tap on the door, and Ryan and I shift away from each other guiltily, even though we aren't actually touching each other, or even close enough to touch.

"Dinner, children," Mrs. Daley says tiredly before moving away.

"After you," Ryan mutters, holding the door open a moment later, frustration in his voice.

CHAPTER 17

Ryan, Louisa Daley, and I make polite, but limited, conversation at dinner before Louisa insists that we *run along now*, refusing to let either of us help with the dishes. As I leave the room behind Ryan, she furiously scrapes leftover food into the trash can while she tries not to let us see her cry. Just business as usual, then.

Disappointment has turned Ryan in on himself again, and we part company outside Lauren's bathroom door without a word said, without a new plan for tomorrow, which leaves me feeling strangely restless, dissatisfied.

Inside her bedroom, I switch off all the lights and pace the pristine carpet for a while, so wired I can't possibly sleep. I go over all of the angles, the dead ends, and it's none for none every time.

Lauren's eyes in her photos seem to follow me around the room. Even in the absolute dark, I can make out every image that contains her—photos of sleepovers, choir friends, pen pals, endless parties forever frozen in time. Her ash-blond hair seems to glow, much as my own reflection does when I pace past the mirrored dresser for the umpteenth time. I have just over a week left to make a difference in Ryan's life before I'm bussed back to whatever dismal place Carmen comes from, or vanish out of this life altogether, into another. And I can't see how either is possible: to resolve things; to leave him.

Maybe Carmen herself is just filler. Some kind of physical way station. I don't want to believe that. I'd like to think that I'm supposed to take something out of this life, or, rather, put something back—for somebody, if not for me.

I throw myself down on the bed, finally, thinking that sleep will evade me this night, and wake suddenly, hours later, paralyzed and choking.

There's a tall figure standing at the foot of the bed, and I can't move a muscle to speak, lift a finger, run.

Is *he* doing it to me? Or is it *her* fear that's holding me down?

I discover that the only things I am able to move are Carmen's eyes. I watch the man drift in place, as if his feet do not touch the ground. So tall, the ceiling almost cannot contain him.

Very little scares me, and yet the shining one—who is so like me he could be my brother, my twin—stands over me with judgment in his eyes, a living flame cupped in his left hand, and I am very afraid.

"I don't believe him," he says, as if refuting something I have just said aloud.

Light shines out of every pore of his body as if he's made of it. His voice is at once so terrible, so beautiful, like thunder advancing from a great distance, a bright bugle call, that I cannot believe Ryan can be sleeping just a few yards away and not hear him.

"*You* can't have *changed*." The stranger's tone is incredulous. "It isn't in you; you were always so adamantine, so . . . inflexible."

I want to scream at him to stop speaking in riddles, but it's as if I'm fixed to the bed by a force field of energy so powerful I cannot make my corded neck work. It is almost worse than my fear of heights, this feeling of utter entombment, Carmen's skin and bones a living shroud in which I am tightly bound. The sensation of being buried alive is at once so powerful and so terrifying that I feel tears spring to her eyes and roll down her frozen features.

Don't do this to me! I wail inside her head as sweat breaks out upon her skin, drenching the white sheets on which we lie. Carmen's eyes widen in fear as we, together, struggle to focus on the being at the foot of the bed.

The burning man moves so swiftly, so imperceptibly, that he's suddenly beside me, on Carmen's left, close enough to touch, if touch were permitted me. Light seems to leak from him in wisps, in errant curls that blur, then fade, into the cool air of Lauren's bedroom. His raiment is of such a bright white that I am blinded as to detail, can only perceive him in outline. Yet I know I have seen him before—even before the other night, when I glimpsed him poised silently beside the roadway. And I realize that once I knew him when I was truly alive and inhabiting my own skin. How I know this, I cannot be sure.

Bending low, he whispers in a voice to rend steel, to

rend stone, "I wanted to see for myself how you have 'changed.' It seems that he has overreached himself, as usual, in his description of you. I see no indication of a shift."

He turns away from me, as if aggrieved, or disappointed. Prepared to vanish back into whatever vortex he stepped out of.

There is a slight lessening of the strange pressure that binds me to Lauren's bed, and I gasp, despite myself, "Uri?" Something subterranean and unheralded in me recognizing something in him.

The tall figure stiffens, turns back quickly. Bends again to inspect me, as if I am a curio, an oddity, from another age.

His voice is like a muted roar, like waves breaking across all the world's oceans in tandem, a thunderclap to split the skies. "What—did—you—*say?*"

I know I should feel fear; I have been cautioned— by Luc, more than once—to be fearful. But that does not even begin to describe what is in my heart.

The being, Uri, raises his left hand, the living flame cupped in it, the better to see her, the better to see *me* within. Plays it across Carmen's unremarkable features,

182

her slight figure stretched out beneath the covers of Lauren's bed.

His lip curls. *So puny, so mortal.* I can almost read his thoughts.

I could always read his thoughts.

"*Uri,*" I cry again, as if I am drowning. "I *know* you."

And for a moment, it is as if an invisible hand is at my throat, crushing Carmen's windpipe until the room turns black at the edges, purple in my sight, the outline of the physical world wavering.

I am suddenly fearful that it may be possible to die in another's body, and I choke out, "You—don't—scare—me. You—never—*did*."

"Liar," says the figure of power. "I can *smell* your human fear. The intervening years have made you weak. Perhaps he was right. You *have* changed, if only to become even *less* than you were."

There are those strange emphases again, and I struggle to draw breath into the girl's body and at the same time comprehend his meaning.

He laughs harshly. "How would we have been able to keep you from him at every turn, if that were not the case?"

He laughs again at that. And, subtly, the energy in the room—the strange, sapping power—increases until the air fairly crackles with it, and I am made rigid, as if electrified by live current. Helpless with longing for movement, for air, for what once was. We were friends, I am sure of it. We laughed; we were equals.

"We ruled the world," he says softly, as if he has read it from my mind, and I know it for the truth.

"Bully," I manage to gasp out.

"Traitor," he replies swiftly, menace in his voice.

The word makes no sense to me, my recall having inconveniently hit a wall.

For an unguarded moment he relaxes his absolute dominion over me, and in that instant, I reach out and grab his hand, like someone going under for the last time.

It is white, his skin, like marble or alabaster, without flaw, and smooth as fired glass or porcelain. Unlined on any surface.

I turn his palm over, and see that Carmen's small hand is lost in it, when the burning begins. Quickly it engulfs her left arm, her torso, all of her, until we are incandescent, rigid in fiery glory.

Uri looks down on us . . . with pity? Compassion?

We burn, *burn*, and our mouth is stretched wide to scream, to bring the walls of this house down, when I see, I see—two great human armies doing battle on a desert plain; beings like Uri among them, above them, on the ramparts of the beleaguered city, doing nothing save watch as hundreds go down, armored and on horseback, on foot. Called to their deaths by blaring horn; a tide of human blood sinking into the unforgiving sand as the watchers do nothing.

Uri, suspended, like a star, above the dome of a great stone mosque, the walls of a sprawling pink desert fort at sunset, the keep of a floating palace haunted by music and the scent of jasmine, the peak of the tallest mountain in the world, the bell tower of a city overrun by plague and death. Uri, falling from the sky yet landing lightly upon the surface of the earth. Uri, passing like a spirit through the bodies of a magnitude without leaving any sensation of his passage. Uri, in a thousand improbable places, yet bending the laws of nature with ease.

Then the years peel back—or do they run forward? —as cities are raised, then sacked, then raised again. Always the new upon the old—or the old upon the new —until pattern, memory, coherence all waver and blur with the rapid passage of time. As I watch through his eyes, the sun and moon streak across the sky continually as fires, famines, wars destroy cities. Civilizations—both celebrated and forgotten—begin to snake out across the surface of the world as vines are wont to do, buildings grow more opulent, more complex, ever taller, like plants reaching toward the sun. We traverse continents, seas, forests, mountains, vast ice floes—experience all of this together, strangely conjoined—as seasons change, and all that is around us alters then decays then alters again. Always and everywhere, the faces of millions— of every creed, color, age, station—wither and become as dust, and among them walk the shining ones, ever watchful yet held apart. Unseen by any save their own kind. Rarely moved to intervene.

Time bends, sound, light, distance, perspective, and all around me the shifting world and everything in it. Until, for an instant, I see, I see—Uri and seven brethren arrayed against *me*—all beautiful, all terrible, their instruments of power raised high—and behind them, a glorious multitude in white, the great universe wheeling and turning about us. Planets, stars, suns, moons, the greater and lesser bodies fly by; comets, black holes, supernovas, strange fissures in time and space twist and curl overhead like a painted, yet living, ever-changing dome.

Home.

The word catches in me.

I know this is a true memory, one of my earliest, for beside me I *sense* Luc—my heart leaping—another shining multitude arrayed at *our* backs, the two of us the epicenter of something vast, a conflagration waiting to happen, an ache in time, a breath suspended.

Then I *see* him, my beloved—like a lion, like a sun god when he walks—as if I am reliving the moment, as if the moment is now. And before I can turn to him, speak, lay my hands upon him in fearful gratitude for the miracle of such restoration—how long have I waited for this? *How long?*—I hear him say, "Then, as an act of faith—of *goodwill*—shall we call it—take that which is most precious to me." His tone is final, without emotion, a death knell. "I permit it."

And then I feel searing pain in my left hand, the original pain, the wound that begot all wounds, all misfortunes thereafter, and then the world goes white and blank.

And I am rendered deaf, dumb, and blind. For all purposes, *dead* to that shining multitude, removed from them in an instant, cut off forever, as if a limb amputated, never to return.

And I am lost again, as I am suddenly hurled out of contact with the being, Uri, who is clearly shaken.

"Exaudi nos, Domine," he whispers as he looks at the place where our two hands were joined, as if a new scar might have formed there. It could have been days or mere seconds that we touched.

"You of all people should know how it works, Uri," I reply. "The Lord only helps those who help themselves, remember?" As I say the words, I discover that I am finally able to sit upright. I hug Carmen's bony knees gingerly as I look up into Uri's beautiful countenance, startle a crooked smile from him.

"*That*, my friend, is where we differ in philosophical outlook," he says, a touch ruefully. "A shift has indeed occurred, it would seem. Disturbingly, my informant does not prove false."

Time is short in every sense, so while I am able, while the creature's mood nears benevolence (as much as one such as he is able to feel benevolence), I say raggedly,

"Then help me this time? I need to find her. I need you to intervene. Just this once. For me. Such a small thing, brother."

I struggle to keep my tone even, still wondering why, so many times, he and his brethren watched while all around them were lost or destroyed, transfigured forever. And still they stood by and did nothing when they had the power in them to do anything . . . everything.

Uri pauses perceptibly, and I watch the light bleed from him in little drifts, in errant curls of pure energy.

When he finally answers, his voice is gentle. "It has already been decided. You know this as well as I do. Everything now and to be has a past cause that may be known or deduced and from which all consequence flows. *We* are the masters of natural law through which all events may be viewed and given meaning. Further are we above all beasts and all men, the first caste, the foremost. Therefore, intervention is pointless. The girl is already lost and gone. She is nothing. Forget her."

The answering fury I feel is swift and unexpected.

"Surely, *we* are not the only ones with liberty!" I cry. "*They* exercise free will every day, every second of their lives. The world is *chaos*, as are all who live in it.

Nothing is fixed from moment to moment. I have seen it. Lived it! How can you deny it?"

Uri's face is impassive. "Consider your current state. Does *she* demonstrate any such freedom of will? Everything she does is a direct consequence of *your* actions."

For a moment I am speechless. It's a good point. When tested, it does not seem to yield.

"But she is *constrained*," I rasp out finally.

"Because we *willed* it," he replies calmly. "We have always and ever been the masters of their fate, and our own. With one only having higher authority over us all. Free will is an illusion. You would do well to remember it, if nothing else. Perhaps he *is* right. Perhaps you have altered beyond all recognition."

I am almost begging. "But she is likely still alive, brother."

As I say the word again, *brother*, Uri's eyes narrow and soften momentarily.

"If you will not free me," I sigh, "at least do this one thing I ask of you."

His expression is unreadable once more as he shakes his head, his long, brown hair falling freely about his shoulders. Every strand straight, even and perfectly the same. "I cannot do it. Do not ask it of me." Is there sadness in his words? Pity?

"Will not, more likely." Frustration roughens my tone. "What *are* you?"

When he replies, his bell-like voice holds a note of challenge. "No. The question is, what are *you*?"

We glare at each other fiercely, both freezing as we hear someone ascend the staircase outside Lauren's room. Heavy footsteps head down the hallway before pausing and retracing their way to her door. There is a soft tapping.

"Carmen?" It is Stewart Daley's voice, weariness in it. "Is everything all right? May I come in?"

I see the handle turn a fraction, clockwise.

"I'm fine!" I squeak out, loud enough for the man outside to hear. "It's nothing. Just a bad dream. Sorry I disturbed you."

Did he often stand there, like that, when his daughter was home and asleep in her bed?

For a long, poised moment, he does not move away, only the door between him and my shining interlocutor.

Even as Mr. Daley says, "Well, good night, then,"

and begins to move away down the hall, Uri says softly, "Luc wants you for his own. He cannot be trusted. Do not allow past feeling to interfere with your judgment. Do not fall to him or all will be lost. You may not know it, will not necessarily thank us, but it has always been for you, *always*."

Before I can reach out and hold him to me for another fleeting instant, before I can tell him I *want* to be found by Luc, now more than ever, Uri's outline wavers and splinters into infinitesimal motes of light that wink out and are gone. And I am hit again by a wave of loneliness so vast that it feels for a second as if I am the one who has broken apart and cannot be put back together.

I send fury, despair, grief shooting straight into the night sky, like a beacon.

Let someone hear it! I scream silently. *Exaudi me, Domine.*

I realize anew the value of what I might have lost, and it is vast.

Who am I? whispers that inner voice that is never silent. *What am I capable of?*

CHAPTER 18

Despite what Ryan told me the night before, I am determined to lay hands on Gerard Masson at this morning's rehearsal and sift through his innermost thoughts. If he is as blameless as the lamb, something in me will recognize it. I know now that guilt will rise to the surface like oil on the water, like blood. I just need to look for it.

My encounter with the being called Uri last night confirms it. There is an inexplicable power in me that will not be denied, not even by something, someone, not of this world.

The meaning of his warning, however, continues to elude me. Random aspects of his words return to trouble me as I drag Carmen's glittery pink hairbrush haphazardly through the tangles in her hair, shrug my way into her doll-sized clothes.

What has always been for me?

And *why*?

And what did Luc's act of goodwill serve to prove? Permit?

I chase the answers down the unreliable pathways of Carmen's brain even though I know they are not there; they are buried somewhere within *me*, the ghost-in-the-machine.

When I recall again that moment of blank white pain, I feel a terrible numbness, the echoes of some deeper grief whose cause I cannot yet bring to the surface. And though *I* cannot cry tears—*was not formed to do so*, corrects that small voice inside—I find tears on Carmen's face as I apply cherry-pink lip gloss carefully to the tiny bow of her mouth, dust the bronzing powder I found at the bottom of her carryall across the bridge of her small, fine nose.

Tears for me, cried by a stranger.

By the time I head down to breakfast, Ryan has already left the house on some willful errand known only to himself. I find myself missing him already. Beneath the calm surface that Carmen presents to the world, I beat myself up about it. People in your situation, my inner voice informs me dryly, should not form attachments. It's a given.

You think I don't know that?

Could have fooled me.

Smart-ass.

As I rise from the table after Carmen's usual meager breakfast—her body a machine requiring very little fuel —Mr. Daley surprises me by offering me a lift to school.

Louisa Daley's dark eyes settle on mine for a long moment before she says, "Have a good day," in a neutral voice, turning away from her husband.

"We've hardly looked after you," Mr. Daley says apologetically, as he holds open the front door, beckons me out ahead of him. "And here's almost a week gone. It's the least I can do."

What did he hear last night when he was poised outside Lauren's bedroom door? I am immediately all caution.

"Well, that's very kind." I put shyness in my voice, hanging my head a little. "But after you, Mr. Daley. The dogs, you know."

"Ah, yes," he replies, looking at me quizzically for a fraction too long.

He's so like Ryan, I can see the son's future mapped out in the older man's face. *Let there be no more suffering in it*, I think. And it's almost a prayer.

Mr. Daley disposes of the baying hounds in the usual manner, and installs me in the front passenger seat, both of us absurdly careful not to touch each other. I suppose I will have to reach out to him again at some point, to be absolutely certain. But I'll tackle the little music teacher first. The echoes of Mr. Daley's mental anguish are still too fresh in my mind for comfort, and I trust Ryan.

Perhaps too much. Trust has been so long absent from my weird limbo existence that even acknowledging the fact is like a leap of faith.

Stewart Daley makes inconsequential small talk as we drive across town to school. I make the appropriate noises in return. Tell him politely how much I am enjoying my stay in his bucolic town, lying like the professional that I am, the leaf-shaped air freshener swinging like a pendulum between us.

As he drops me off just outside Paradise High's main

gate, he says approvingly, "It seems you've made a good impression on my wayward son, young lady. Ryan's even talking about heading back to school in the spring, and I like to think you've had something to do with that. Maybe he's finally giving up on this . . . nonsense of his."

I turn, on the point of swinging my legs out of the car. "It isn't nonsense, Mr. Daley," I reply seriously.

I almost touch him, think better of it, withdraw Carmen's small hand, take a firmer grip on the backpack between my feet. Later, maybe. I'm no coward. But it's like what Pavlov did to that poor dog, you know? Once burned . . .

I add reassuringly, "You have to believe she's still out there, that she'll come home. I do."

Immediately, his open, friendly expression shuts down, his eyes go blank. He looks away as he says dully, "That way lies madness, you know? It's what our therapist told us. *If you don't accept she's dead, you don't heal.* We have to 'seal off' the incident. I have to believe he knows what he's doing."

I watch as, to the accompaniment of shouted expletives and blaring horns, Stewart Daley executes a ragged U-turn across two lanes of oncoming school-bound traffic before burning back in the direction of Main Street.

Gerard Masson stops me before I'm about to sit down on the fringes of the soprano section. Around us, people are still taking their chairs all over the room.

"Good morning, Carmen!" he says brightly, one chubby hand on my sleeve.

I pause, staring hard at him. He's a toucher, and it's instinctive; my dislike of being touched, like learned behavior. Plus, he stinks of . . . *alcohol*? His skin exudes an overpowering odor, like the inside of a wine cask. Can no one else smell it? I almost wrench my arm away, then I remember.

Should I do it now? Reach into his head right here and take what knowledge I need from his mind?

"Good morning, Mr. Masson," Tiffany interrupts loudly, her best sweetness-and-light game face on. As usual, she hasn't missed a trick. She's like a tabloid reporter camped outside my gates, always on my case. "Is there something you wanted to tell us before the rehearsal starts?" she adds. "Something *we*—the sopranos—need to work on?"

She looks around at us, bats her tinted eyelashes, queen of all she freakin' surveys.

Wretched Tiffany and her big, carrying voice. Every soprano's suddenly focused on the fact that Mr. Masson's still holding on to me, and I can't go into some kind of off-the-wall trance, with Tiffany's eyes—not to mention all the rest—boring into me like . . . well, lasers.

Despite the slight tremor in Gerard Masson's fingers, his voice is controlled. "Well, no, Tiffany. The sopranos are doing just fine. Nothing the general rehearsal can't fix. I just wanted to corner young Carmen here to offer her a special solo in the upcoming concert. She's quite the revelation! Really come out of her, uh, ah, shell." As he speaks, his fingers dig into my sleeve momentarily. "I thought something still in the ecclesiastical mold, Carmen," he says—and I'd like to step back, but I've got nowhere to go—"but a little lighter, to leaven the vigorousness of the Mahler. Perhaps something by John Rutter? Or a Willcocks arrangement?"

Who? I have to remind myself sharply to shut Carmen's mouth.

He beams at me, and I hope Carmen's face is registering enthusiasm, though, in truth, I have neither the time nor any interest in committing more music to memory. Carmen, the real Carmen, would probably be feeling euphoria right about now. Followed in rapid order—and I'd put good money on it—by crippling self-doubt.

There's no letup from Tiffany. She comes right back with "Carmen and I often perform duets at St. Joseph's. We have *plenty* prepared. Would you believe one of them's actually a Rutter composition—you'd know it, I'm sure, Mr. Masson—'Angels' Carol.' It would be perfect to round out the program—"

"In fact," I cut in quickly, "why not let Tiffany do the solo? She's had *loads* more experience. She'd be a natural for a killer finale, right, Tiff?"

I feel a sudden twinge of discomfort—like a stitch in my side—see Delia and Marisol lock eyes in disbelief. Tiffany's expression dissolves, unflatteringly, into shock.

"Why, thank you for your kind offer, Tiffany," Gerard Masson returns quickly, still standing way too close for comfort, "but I have a number of specific works in mind that I think would really bring out Carmen's particular gifts. I thought we might *open* with you, my dear," he says, returning his full attention to me eagerly. "Give the audience something uplifting to begin the evening with before we hit them with everything we've got, so to speak. Can you stay behind after tonight's rehearsal and we'll get down to brass tacks? There'll be a few extra rehearsals involved as well—all one-on-one with me, of course, there's no time to waste—but you seem a quick study, it should pose no extra difficulty for you, I'm sure. I've already cleared it with Fiona Fellows, who is all for you taking on more responsibility. Said it would do you good."

I bet she did, I think grimly. What can I do but tightly nod my head?

My answer secured, the man finally lets go of me and sails ahead to the podium, crying, "Let's mix it up this morning, people! We've got one more week after today to knock this thing on the head!" As he says this, he shoots me a conspiratorial wink. It doesn't go unnoticed.

"You're so *two-faced*," Tiffany says angrily, before turning a cold shoulder on me.

Conditions in the rehearsal space are almost as arctic, and the prospect of having to enter this room and start all over again the following Monday makes me groan out loud.

Mr. Masson continues, deliberately upbeat. "Today, Miss Dustin and I will take the general chorus ladies —choirs one and two—in the assembly hall." The "ladies" in question roll their eyes and bitch loudly among themselves. "Mr. Barry and Miss Fellows will take the general chorus men in the seniors' rec room."

"Over my dead body!" snorts one wag loudly, to accompanying laughter.

"*I solisti,*" Mr. Masson says in a hammy Italian accent, ignoring the joker with a fixed smile, "will have some special one-on-one time with Mr. Stenborg. He's had a few good ideas about how to sharpen up the boys' entry into Figure Thirty. You have to admit it's still pretty sloppy. I've asked him to work on individual entries and exits with each of you."

"Spencer, Spencer, Spencer," someone interjects, to more laughter.

I scan the room and pick out Spencer easily in the thin lineup of tenors. He's blushing a fiery red as usual, and dressed again like a mail-order-catalogue model, which does him no favors.

Mr. Masson frowns. "Now, now, we're not singling out anybody for punishment here. From where I'm standing, *everyone* could use a little work. Carmen excepted, of course."

He beams again my way when he says this, the stupid idiot, and plenty of people begin to whisper, craning their necks to see my reaction.

"She's been note perfect and unimpeachable since she 'rediscovered' her groove," he says, "which is more than I can say about the rest of you."

His tone is light, to keep the sting out of his words, but Tiffany flushes an unbecoming maroon, because, let's face it, she's been right on the money, too. Only no one's noticed lately, and that's got to be a first for her.

"Crush alert," someone hisses behind me, and people around me roll their eyes and laugh.

The expression on my face doesn't change. I don't even turn around. Because, unlike the real Carmen, I don't care what people think.

"Soloists, follow Paul, if you please," Gerard Masson finishes. He stumbles slightly against the microphone as he steps away from the conductor's podium, but only I seem to notice it.

Tiffany's the first to her feet, hugging her music to her chest and chatting animatedly to Paul Stenborg's clean, Nordic profile before the rest of us have even gathered our things. The seven of us follow the handsome choirmaster into the same room the sopranos occupied the day before, and draw up seats close around the piano—Tiffany front and center as usual; me out on the margin, nearest the door; Spencer settling in shyly beside me.

He raises his eyebrows wordlessly as if to say: *Here we go again.* I return the gesture.

I'll have to get to Gerard Masson during one of my "special" rehearsals. It will almost be worth being stuck in a practice room with the guy just to know for sure.

CHAPTER
19

"Now, isn't this cozy?" says Paul Stenborg gravely, but with a twinkle in his eyes, as he plays a loud piano chord with a flourish and turns half around on the piano stool to face us, sunlight glinting off his steel frames, his artfully tousled hair.

He works patiently on the entry to Figure 30 with the boys, drilling them on their individual weaknesses, before attending to the handful of entries that are led off by a bass or an alto.

"*Lumen accende sensibus,*"—kindle our senses with light—he sings at one point, shadowing Delia note for note during a difficult passage around Figure 33.

I sit straighter in astonishment. His voice is like liquid

amber—light, pure, supple. Itself wholly remarkable and more beautiful by far than Delia's pedestrian instrument. A countertenor's voice, an angel's voice, a complete show stopper. The man is a mystery box, clearly, more than just great window dressing. I wonder again how he could be content with all . . . this.

"Amorem cordibus," he corrects Spencer gently a moment later, rolling his *R*s extravagantly. "Your vowels are far too flat. This is a *romance* language, Spencer Grady. The mother of all romance languages. The phrase is literally begging you to put some *heart* into it."

He laughs at his little joke. Only I get it.

Strangely, Paul does not look my way all morning. Instead, he's incredibly attentive to Tiffany and the other girls; at times, he's even almost kind to Spencer, who hardly wriggles in the seat beside me. It's like I'm invisible again. Is he *angry* with me? I can't catch and hold Paul's gaze, and I'm intrigued, almost piqued.

Maybe he means for me to be. Whatever, I'm happy to play along. It's giving me time to think. I don't enjoy being the center of attention, never have. Though I can handle it. There's a distinct difference.

"Time's almost up, children," Paul says eventually, swinging across the back of the piano seat to face us. "I know that some of you are interested in pursuing a career on the stage beyond high school, and are *more* than competent to do so. . . ." He looks directly at Tiffany and Delia and smiles. And the girls—cast-iron bitches both—actually blush with pleasure. "So since that's the case," he adds, turning back to face the keyboard, "let's see how much of our good work this morning has actually sunk in. I'm going to take it from the top, and you're really going to have to keep up. The weak *will* fall by the wayside," he warns with a soft laugh. "And there will be no mercy."

I flinch at the word.

Flinch again as Paul strikes the first chord of the piano accompaniment. He's true to his promise, working his way through the piece at a flying tempo, only stopping occasionally to beat in Tiffany, Delia, Spencer, the other two boys, with his right hand while his left continues to dance across the keyboard.

He doesn't extend me the same courtesy, merely barking "Figure Seven," "Figure Ten," "Figure Twelve," and so forth whenever a phrase begins with my part, the first soprano. There is no letup, no time to breathe, and even *I'm* being taxed to my limits.

"Good," he mutters from time to time, head bent over the keyboard. "Good."

It's Mahler on speed. And it's great that I know the music sideways, because I need to. The others—save for Tiffany, who sees only what she wants to see, hears only what she wants to hear—follow our interplay with uneasy awe, turn the pages furiously, struggle to keep time, maintain focus, especially in the places where I am absent from the score.

Near the end, near my last crazed *Gloria* around Figure Ninety-one, even Tiffany's about to break down, has a suspicious sheen in her eyes as Paul roars at her, "Double forte, girl. This is no time to run out of steam. Do that in concert at Carnegie Hall and you—will—never—work—*again*."

The final *Patri*—Father—rips through the room, all nine bars of it, and when we're done, breathing heavily like we've just run the race of our lives, we look at each other in amazement. Spencer wipes his mouth with the back of one pudgy hand, Tiffany's face is high with color, and Delia is audibly puffing.

"Now, *that's* a rehearsal." Paul grins, slamming his score shut with satisfaction. "Let's head back to the others now and give them hell."

A little shakily, we rise from our seats, clutching our music. I'm about to lead everyone from the room when Paul says quietly, almost as an afterthought, the question in danger of being lost in the scrape of chairs being pushed back, "Carmen? A word. Walk with me?"

Tiffany shoots me a hard look and sweeps out of the room, Delia at her side; Spencer glances back at me and Paul a little uncertainly as we trail the group back to the assembly hall.

"I'll admit, I wasn't pleased at the way Gerard singled you out at the beginning of the rehearsal," Paul says, his voice pitched so that only he and I can hear. "He's always been guilty of playing favorites a little too much. It causes . . . talk."

I look at him inquiringly, sure Lauren was one of those favorites.

"It's unprofessional," he continues grimly. "And I don't agree with his approach. Jealousies inevitably arise. But in any case, *that*, my girl"—he smiles at me for the first time that morning—"was another test. And you performed *beautifully*. Those two"—his voice is slightly scornful as he inclines his golden head at Tiffany's back, Delia's—"are mere cattle. Ordinary. But you . . ."

He breaks into a grin of open approval, a light flush high on his extraordinary cheekbones.

"I wouldn't say Tiffany's exactly . . . ordinary," I cut in, keen to hurry him along. My thoughts are on Gerard Masson. If I have to rote learn a freakin' Christmas carol to get inside the man's head, so be it.

Groups of boys from the male chorus begin to filter into the hallway around us, and Paul Stenborg drops his voice a notch lower. "She's nothing," he insists. "Powerful, yes, I'll give her that. But shrill. Not enough staying power. Good for the opera chorus at most. *You,* however, have what it takes to sing anything, anywhere. I've only encountered a voice like yours a couple of times before in my career, and in my opinion—and I will tell Gerard this; he's asked my views on the subject already—you far outshine them. You are, in a word, *superlative*, my dear. You should never let someone like Tiffany get to you. There's simply no contest."

"Oh?" I say, and feel a sudden twinge of discomfort. *Carmen? Can you hear this?*

"Gerard was right, you know." My gaze shoots back to Paul's animated face at the mention of the man's name again. "That mad, breakneck version of Mahler back there? *He* ordered me to force your hand this morning —and I have to say that you more than exceeded our expectations! He's going to be very excited about what we've achieved this morning. Very excited indeed. Says he has great plans for you."

Gerard Masson's been laying unspoken traps for me? Formulating secret agendas? All this just makes me quicken my step toward the assembly hall. I have to get to him. I have to know.

Beside me, Paul lengthens his stride, keeping up easily as he confides, "Genuine talent like yours is truly, incredibly *rare*." My eyes flash to the back of Spencer's head at the words, but he doesn't hear, or look my way.

"If you say so," I reply as we turn the corner, the corridor suddenly full of students headed the way we are.

There's that weird feeling again, like a stitch in my side, and I can almost hear Carmen begging me not to screw this up for her, not to sell her too short in my quest to find Lauren. For an instant, I'm torn. Lauren first? Or Carmen? Who was I sent here to help?

Paul places a hand on my sleeve, which makes me
look down in surprise. I'd almost forgotten he was there.
"Do you want to grab a coffee after today's rehearsal?
I can give you some pointers on how to handle Gerard
—who can be a little . . . insistent," he says delicately.
"Perhaps go over some of your career options? I have
contacts—better than any Gerard may offer you."

When I don't respond, he says a little more sharply,
"I don't think you're really hearing me. . . ."

And it's true. I'm no longer listening, suddenly can't
even hear what he's saying, because I've just caught sight
of Ryan standing beside the entrance to the assembly
hall. His eyes telling me that he needs me.

Paul makes a small noise of surprise, or protest, as I take
Carmen's sleeve out of his grasp.

People stare as I push through the crowded corridor
in Ryan's direction. I hear the whispers: "What's *he*
doing here?" "When's the last time anyone saw *him* at
school?"

I put my hands on his shirtsleeves. I can tell from
his face something has happened. There's a look in his

eyes I haven't seen there before. Like the death of hope. Something fatal to his resolve.

Plenty of people are taken aback at my familiarity, and heads swivel so fast in our direction that there's a real risk of a general case of whiplash. It's more reason for people to talk about Carmen, about him, but I don't care. Seeing him like this has done something funny to my heart.

"What's happened?" I say breathlessly. "Have they found her?"

My touch seems to bring his splintering gaze back into focus, his eyes so dark I can't see his pupils. Shock. He shakes his head, his long dark fringe falling over his eyes.

"No," he says, and his voice sounds strange, remote. "But someone else just got taken. In Little Falls. It's on all the local news bulletins. She was a singer, too, a soprano. A little older. All the hallmarks of Lauren's abduction. Happened over the weekend—they were trying to keep it quiet, but the media got wind of it. Almost two years to the day. The media are already linking them together. You were right about that part, the singing thing. I shouldn't have set so much store by a stupid . . . dream." He swallows hard.

There are students standing close by, listening to us unashamedly, their mouths open. I dimly register Paul Stenborg moving past us into the assembly hall, his eyes dark with unexpected anger. I suppose he thinks I'm rude, but I don't care. Carmen can wait, the competing agendas of a bunch of small-town music teachers can wait, when Ryan looks this way.

I pull him down the hallway by his sleeve, and out of the building, so we can talk. The harsh light outside accentuates his pallor, the dark beneath his eyes, in his eyes.

"Does it mean she's dead?" he asks bleakly, and Carmen's heart does a weird flip. It must be costing him a lot to say this.

I parry the question, try to get him to look at me. "What does your instinct tell you?"

"Instinct tells me she's dead. Instinct tells me the sick bastard got tired of her and traded 'up.'" His voice cracks as he throws himself down on the front steps of an empty portable classroom nearby, puts his head in his hands, puts his hands over his eyes.

"I don't feel anything," he whispers after a long silence. "That's the problem."

I have to resist the urge to stroke his hair. It's a new feeling for me and it makes me edgy. Why this need to touch him so often? I *never* initiate contact. It's unnerving.

"It works both ways," I reply cautiously. "If something really bad had happened, wouldn't you think you'd have *felt* it?"

Ryan raises his head sharply, considers this for a moment. "Yeah, I guess I would have. Either way. You're right."

"So what do you want me to do?" I cross my arms tightly and wait for his answer.

He screws up his face. "I don't know. Go for a drive, look around. Hold my hand." He looks up at me, looks away, his fringe falling back over his eyes.

He doesn't mean that last part, I tell myself sternly. *It's just a figure of speech. I need to hold firm.* Though it's almost as if I can feel myself . . . falling.

"If we don't act quickly," he mutters over the soundtrack of my internal dialogue, "she's going to suffer the same fate as Lauren. We can't let that happen." He suddenly unfurls his long, lean frame and bounds up with a new energy. "I'm parked on the other side of the admin building," he calls back over his shoulder. "Come on."

When I don't move, he stops and strides back impatiently. "Sometimes I forget you're not from here. *Come on.*" He holds his hand out to me.

I don't take it. But not because I don't want to.

He shrugs. "Up to you," he says curtly, walking off again. I have to trot to keep up.

As we head out through the school gates in his white, rusting four-wheeler, I look at his breathtaking profile and think how it is that I don't. I don't ever forget that I'm not from here.

CHAPTER
20

We stop at a gas station on the outskirts of Little Falls and buy a paper. Singing has made me so hungry that I ransack the poorly stocked candy counter with Carmen's modest stash of spending money, buying one of almost everything.

When we get back in the car, we pore over the front page together, our heads so close I'm almost leaning on him.

Little Falls woman, Jennifer Appleton, 19, university student majoring in fine arts and vocal performance, missing. Police hold grave fears for her safety.

Ryan regards me with disgust as crumbs fall onto the page. "How can you eat at a time like this?" he exclaims, shaking the paper clear.

"Stress makes me hungry." I shrug, already crumpling up my second candy wrapper and reaching for a third. I unwrap it and begin cramming it gracelessly into my mouth.

"I heard you sing," he says, giving me a strange look. "I knew it was your voice, don't ask me how, even though I couldn't see you and didn't know where it was coming from. Actually, it seemed to be coming from everywhere at once. And it sounded, uh, kind of effortless. Lauren used to joke about how tone deaf I am, but you were . . ."

"What?" I grin through a mouthful of chocolate and peanuts, sure they're all over my teeth. "Barely adequate? Hopelessly grating?"

He rolls his eyes, thinking I'm fishing for compliments. "Pretty incredible, actually. But you'd know that. Lauren would hate me for saying it, because she's always been known as the primo singing prodigy around these parts, but you're *way* better than she is. Better than anyone I've ever heard before. Hard to believe a voice like that can come out of a body like . . ." He looks down at the paper quickly and smoothes it out again. "But what would I know?"

"You and me both," I say, making light of the weird alchemy that is Carmen Zappacosta at the present juncture. I throw candy wrapper number three on the floor and bring his attention back to the story on Jennifer Appleton. "This says she returned to her hometown to perform at her cousin's wedding and disappeared sometime after returning to her parents' place from the reception."

"It's the first time she's been back at all since she left school." Ryan frowns. "She was just doing this as a favor. Says here she's in line for a scholarship at one of the big city opera houses when she graduates at the end of next year. Earmarked for greatness."

I feel that twinge of discomfort again. Carmen? I know now it's something she must want for herself, and I feel that momentary guilt again. That I'm in there batting for Lauren, for Ryan, and not for her.

Or maybe you're just batting for yourself, says that evil voice inside me.

I shift uncomfortably in my seat. There's probably a

bit of truth in that. I grimace as the weird stitch pounds away in my side.

"Physical description?" I ask through my teeth.

"Brunette," he replies distractedly, reading ahead.

We stare at the small, grainy shot of Jennifer Appleton: a smiling, round-faced young woman with glasses and long wavy hair.

"Says here she's tall," I comment.

Ryan frowns. "Lauren's short, only a little bigger than you are. Plus, this girl's older. They're total physical opposites. Maybe we're all jumping to conclusions about there being some kind of connection. . . ."

It's my turn to frown as I race ahead through the article. "Not if you read the crime scene description. It tallies with what I've"—Ryan looks at me sharply— "heard from, uh, various sources," I finish lamely.

He shakes his head disgustedly, then scans the paragraph I've just read. "No signs of forced entry, blood everywhere, a syringe taken away for toxicology tests. Jennifer's father drove her home, then returned to the reception. Hours later, mother and father come back to find her gone. The physical evidence seems to stop at the front gate. Same as for Lauren. The perp was well prepared; very likely wore gloves and shoe covers to explain the lack of DNA at the scene. It's like she vanished into thin air after the psycho got her outside. No tire prints, no witnesses. Someone with local knowledge likely to be involved . . ."

He stares ahead through the fly-struck windshield while I read on, well into candy bar number four. The second to last paragraph makes me grip his shoulder hard.

"What?" he says in surprise.

I point wordlessly, and he reads aloud:

The spokesman for the Appleton family, Laurence Barry, is the director of music at Little Falls Academy and minister of the Little Falls Anglican Church. Reverend Barry was the celebrant at Julia Castle's wedding, and a former teacher of the missing woman. He has appealed to anyone with information to come forward.

Ryan shakes his head. "I don't get you."

"He was there today," I explain. "At the rehearsal.

He's been at *every* rehearsal. Mr. Barry's the old guy, from the karaoke bar?"

Ryan's face clears as understanding dawns.

"He might have met Lauren the same way," I add. "In fact, I'm sure of it. The Little Falls, Port Marie, and Paradise music students apparently get together for cozy shindigs all the time. Lauren was frequently the headline act. All this time I've been focused on Gerard Masson, but maybe Laurence Barry's the missing link. Not many people would have known Jennifer was back. And there's a *church*."

Ryan starts the engine, throws the car into reverse. "Let's go for that drive," he says grimly.

"So that's it?" I say.

We're parked a block away from the Appletons' residence. There's still crime-scene tape forming a loose cordon outside the small timber home. One police car, its lights flashing silently, stands outside, and its burly occupants redirect local traffic and sightseers as we watch.

The scene is repeated outside the wedding and reception venue—a historic homestead on the Little Falls–Port Marie Road.

"Not a lot we can do here during daylight," Ryan muses. "But there's something we know that they don't. My money's on the church, anyway. Right dream, wrong place of worship."

He turns the car back in the direction of town, and we park half a block away from the front boundary of the Little Falls Anglican Church, which is deserted.

The sign out front reads: HE WANTS YOU FOR HIS OWN.

The words cause instant goose flesh on Carmen's skin. They echo the very words Uri threw at me before he did his nifty vanishing trick.

"Cheerful," I say, struggling to keep my voice controlled. "Could be appropriate, in the circumstances. Think Mr. Barry's doing a little advertising?"

Ryan, already getting out of the car, grimaces at my lame attempt at humor. "See anything that looks like the rectory?"

I shake my head, take a steadying breath. "But it could be around the back."

We split up, going through the small parking lot out front; Ryan heading right toward the church, me heading left toward the church hall.

About five minutes later, Ryan gives a piercing whistle.

Like the residence at the Paradise First Presbyterian Church, Laurence Barry's place is a modest, brick one-story building. But it's actually located inside the church grounds, and this time there's some kind of external entry point at the rear of the house that's covered over by a double-padlocked trapdoor made of rusting steel. Ryan hurries back to the car for his backpack as I take a closer look.

Confident Laurence Barry's still back at the rehearsal where I left him, I crouch down and bang on the trapdoor with the heel of my hand. "Hello?" I call out. "Lauren?"

Though I strain to hear anything, anything at all, there's nothing but the wind stirring tree branches, a bird taking wing at the disturbance.

"Jennifer?"

Still no sound. But there could be plenty of reasons for that, all bad. I sit back on my haunches.

Ryan falls to his knees on the ground beside me, hands me the flashlight, and claws through his pack for a bolt cutter. "This is the place, I know it," he says, breathing unevenly. "Everything fits."

Privately, I have to agree; there's something about the way the complex is set up, where the parking lot is, the church. The physical layout seems to correlate eerily with Ryan's dream.

He snaps one padlock swiftly, then the second, stuffs the bolt cutter back into his bag. He swings the trapdoor open and I hand him back the flashlight, wondering what we are about to find. There are concrete stairs leading down into the darkness. We look at each other with wide eyes. This could be it.

I want to hold his hand so badly, I have to jam both of mine under my armpits.

Ryan shrugs his backpack on and puts a foot on the first step.

But then we hear the rumble of a car pulling up the narrow driveway that loops past the church, continuing onward to the private residence we are in the process of breaking into. We freeze for an instant, before scrambling clumsily to close the trapdoor together without a sound.

It's close. In his panic, Ryan almost loses his grip on the door, and Carmen's got as much lifting power as a ten-year-old. I almost crush her fingers as the edge of the door drops shut with an audible clang. I rearrange the broken padlocks hastily so that from a distance they look untampered with.

We crouch in the long grass by the cellar door, and I hear a familiar snatch of Mahler whistled close by. The front screen door of the little house opens just yards away. Someone drops keys, grunts heavily before fishing them up and trying the door again. In the cool breeze, Ryan and I are perspiring heavily. The front door finally closes. Bolts are drawn home.

"*Now*," Ryan hisses, and we run low and quietly down the side of the house, back around the far side of the church hall, in the direction of Ryan's car, hoping we haven't been seen.

"Tonight," Ryan vows as he restarts his car engine, his hands shaking a little. "We'll get them out tonight."

Ryan drops me back at Paradise High on the promise that we'll meet up again at his place after tonight's choir rehearsal.

I grin. "Just watch out for the dogs."

His answering smile is quizzical. "When this is all over, I'll have a few questions for you," he says, waving as he drives off.

When this is all over, I think, a little self-pityingly, *you'll be lucky if Carmen remembers who you are.*

CHAPTER
21

I insinuate myself into my last period chemistry class, squeezing in beside Tiffany just to get a rise out of her. I know she's going to ask, and, for once in her life, Carmen Zappacosta is not going to spill her guts just for a little measly attention. Not on my watch, anyway.

Tiffany manages to look both hurt and scandalized as I calmly open my borrowed textbook. "Where have *you* been?" she snaps. "Everybody saw you. Sneaking around with a virtual *murderer*. Your disappearance didn't exactly go unnoticed, you know. Mr. Masson's pretty pissed, he was looking for you everywhere. And Miss Fellows is about to have you *suspended*—indefinitely."

When I don't reply, leaning forward as if the discussion on migrating electrolytes has to be the most fascinating thing I've ever encountered, Tiffany snipes, "You'll be interested to know that your little vanishing act this morning is already yesterday's news anyway. A killer's on the loose. If I were you, I wouldn't jump into bed with just *anyone.*"

"Who says we did anything in a bed?" I reply casually.

It's enough to shut her up for the rest of the class, though I can feel her practically vibrating with rage beside me.

At four o'clock, Tiffany and I still aren't talking, but we're sitting next to each other in the rehearsal hall as if we're joined at the hip. In frosty silence, we watch the kids bussed in from Little Falls and Port Marie unenthusiastically straggle in for the second rehearsal of the day, the last of the week.

Paul Stenborg flirts easily with Miss Fellows, and the old battle-ax almost smiles, though her gaze turns flinty when it meets mine, signaling bad things in Carmen's future. Miss Dustin stands by wordlessly, looking a little flushed as Paul says something to her before his eyes flick briefly to me and Tiffany, then away.

As Mr. Masson picks up his baton and tries feebly to call us to order—his eyes locating my seated figure with almost comical relief—I catch Laurence Barry staring at me steadily from across the room.

I stare back, so long and unblinkingly that the man finally breaks eye contact. I wonder for one uneasy moment whether he saw Ryan and me running away from his house earlier today. But he doesn't look at me again, and I grow calmer as the session gets under way, although part of me is edgy with the knowledge that I will need to confirm the old man's involvement at rehearsal's end. Via the usual methods.

For the next two hours, I dutifully play Carmen to the hilt, and she's never sounded better. Even Miss Fellows ceases frowning across the hall, because Carmen cannot be faulted. People are leaning forward to get a look at Carmen, some people in the back are even half standing, because Carmen's voice has inspired some kind of general resurgence. Whole phrases of the piece are really starting to come together. It's a win-win for everybody except Tiffany—who's furious.

Carmen's incredible voice cuts through Tiffany's

best efforts to drown us out. There *is* no contest, and suddenly I understand why Tiffany always tries to keep Carmen close, even though she probably hates the girl like poison.

"You think you're so *good*," she snipes, under cover of the increasingly frantic orchestra.

I shrug.

Beyond that, I'm deaf to anything Tiffany or the others have to say. I'm thinking about Ryan, and wondering what he's doing, and yelling at myself for even thinking that when I should be focused on Lauren, on Jennifer, and how to get them out.

We finish at six fifteen, and I look around for Laurence Barry. I'm shocked to discover he's no longer in the room, and when I ask around, I find that no one's seen him in the last half hour. He's already *left*. Does he have some idea that Ryan and I are on to him?

I dodge Miss Fellows—who's actively searching me out like a heat-seeking missile—by hiding in the girls' restroom until I'm sure she's gone, along with just about everyone else. I know that when she finally tracks Carmen down next week, it won't be pretty. Maybe the Lord *will* be kind; maybe I'll be gone by then. I mean,

Carmen's going to have to learn to take care of herself sooner or later.

The hallway is empty when I finally emerge from the restroom, and many of the fluorescents in the classrooms have been turned off. The assembly hall is one of the only remaining oases of light in the entire school complex. I'm about to head back to the Daleys' place when I notice Tiffany's brassy head of hair through the doorway. She's one of the last of the stragglers, loitering with intent— making a beeline for Paul Stenborg by the battered old upright piano near the podium.

The troublemaker in *me* decides to cut in on her dance, just for the fun of it. Hey, there's got to be a first time for everything. Plus, I need some additional information, and Paul might have some background I could use. *Two birds with one stone*, I think, as I stroll over. What could be more perfect?

"Hi, Paul," I say cheerfully.

Tiffany's head whips around in disbelief.

"Hey, Tiff," I add. She's probably been working her way up to this all week.

"What do *you* want?" she barks.

REBECCA LIM

I grin. "Same thing you do."

Paul raises his eyebrows. "Oh, I doubt it," he says. "She was just telling me how she's having trouble with Figure Eighty-three onward and could she have some after-hours, one-on-one coaching. I just told her to follow your lead. I don't think she was very happy with my suggestion."

I frown, flipping quickly in my head through the score I've memorized note for note, word for word, until I reach Figure 83. It begins the last section of the piece that snowballs into the screaming finish—soloists, orchestra, offstage brass, dueling choirs all competing to see who can make the most noise. Paul's right. Tiffany and I sing a lot of that section together on the same notes, and I've never seen any sign of a struggle. There's no way she wouldn't already be note perfect in her quest to always go one higher, faster, better than her arch frenemy.

My expression clears. "We could run through it now, together?" I suggest sweetly. "It would be no trouble, Tiff. I've got plenty of time."

Tiffany's mouth falls open for a moment at having her bluff publicly called. "Ooh!" she huffs, shutting her score with a snap and walking away from Paul and me at the piano.

"Do you want to take a rain check?" Paul calls out mischievously. "I'm always happy to help."

"So am I," I add mildly.

Tiffany gives us both the finger without looking back, and Paul and I burst out laughing. I can tell this is nothing new for him. Catfights and rampaging hormones must come with the territory. I mean, the man's been *stalked*, for Christ's sake. I wonder how he stands it.

Amusement still lighting his pale eyes, Paul asks, "So what can I *really* do for you? We have some unfinished business, my girl. You're a hard woman to pin down. Bolting from this morning's rehearsal really grabbed everyone's attention. It also highlighted how you're way ahead of anyone else out there, and the backbone of this sorry mess. Was that the plan?"

I shake my head, still grinning. "Though Tiffany would tell you differently."

"I bet," he replies. "Is now a good time to grab that coffee?"

"I just need you to answer a couple of quick questions," I say hastily. "We can make a separate date to talk about my career options next week, if you like."

His expression turns into one of intrigued inquiry. "Shoot," he says, shuffling loose piano music into a neat pile with his long-fingered hands, his eyes never leaving mine.

"I'm staying with the Daleys," I say.

"Oh, yes," he replies immediately, taking a seat on the piano stool with his back to the keys, his eyes still on mine. "What a sad, sad situation."

"Yes, yes, it is," I say. "I was just wondering whether Lauren Daley ever met Laurence Barry before she disappeared."

Paul stares at me for a moment, then frowns. "Laurence Barry? Why, certainly. Before you came along and put us all definitively in the shade, Lauren was the star soprano at our joint school concerts. Laurence has been the Little Falls music director since 1969; practically forever to someone as young as you are. He gave her a lot of private coaching, I believe, for the combined concert we held the year she disappeared. Gerard Masson took her lunchtime coaching sessions, but had Laurence take her for the before- and after-school ones because the old man's the opera fanatic. I remember it clearly—that was my first year in the job and Gerard was *raving* about her. Said he'd make her a star by any means at his disposal. I'd just moved here from the Framlingham School."

He beams, as if I should know the name, but it means nothing to me. It must be that fancy city school that Spencer was talking about.

I try to keep my voice even and conversational. "And do you remember a student from Little Falls called Jennifer Appleton? Would she and Lauren have had any connection?"

Paul's expressive mouth turns down. "I hope they catch that monster," he murmurs. "*Of course* I remember Jennifer Appleton. She was one of the remarkable singers I was telling you about. Lauren was the other one." His eyes grow slightly unfocused as he says softly:

> *"Sous le dôme épais*
> *Où le blanc jasmin*
> *Ah! Descendons*
> *Ensemble!"*

His eyes snap back to mine when I continue to look blank. "It's French," he says gently. "*Under the thick dome where the white jasmine . . . Ah! We descend, together!"*

"Uh, okay," I say. Clearly, I was never a fluent French speaker in any past life.

"From Léo Delibes' *Lakmé*," Paul adds helpfully. "Jennifer and Lauren sang the most *incredible* duet. Both of them these tiny little things, one so dark, one so pale. They were a lot like you, actually—delicate-looking but with incredible power in their voices. That's what I was trying to tell you the other day. It's uncanny that I should stumble across *three* of you with such talent, with such similar . . . physicality, all here in 'Paradise' of all places. Fitting, don't you think?" His light eyes hold a look of amused reverie.

He smiles. "Where was I? Oh, yes. Lauren—she'd only just turned sixteen—sang the demanding part of Mallika, and Jennifer, the divine part of Lakmé. A kind of passing of the musical baton from one prodigy to the other, so to speak—it was Jennifer's final year at Little Falls Academy. It's a pity she got so tall and fat. Who would have thought? Anyway, what an incredible night. They blew the audience away, and people around here think music's only for piping into elevators or shopping malls. You should have heard the silence after they finished singing! After everyone regained their senses, the applause didn't stop for at least twenty minutes. They were forced to give *two* encores. No one had ever heard anything like it. Likely never will again. We all knew at least one of them was headed for immortality, if not both."

His eyes are shining with the memory, excitement in his beautiful voice, then his face clouds over. "Then all this happened. It's a weird coincidence, don't you think? The two of them taken? Somehow . . . *collected*?"

Then he shoots me a shrewd look. "But *you* don't think it's a coincidence, do you? You think Laurence had something to do with it. Have you spoken to anyone else about this? It's pretty explosive stuff. Laurence is up there with God around these parts, in more ways than one. Some people think he has a direct line. . . ." The corners of his mouth quirk up a little.

I shake my head. "It's just something I came up with on my own. Just a crazy thought. What would *I* know? I mean, who'd believe me?"

For some reason, I keep Ryan's name out of it. The guy's got no one else looking out for his privacy.

"Who indeed?" Paul says sympathetically. "Well, the man clearly had opportunity," he muses. "He's been tight with the Appleton family since Jennifer's parents were each in their teens, and he was coaching both of the girls before the concert—Jennifer *and* Lauren. But it's still a lot to process. No one's ever fingered Laurence before. It makes a crazy kind of sense, but it won't be popular. You might have stumbled onto something here," he says.

I shake my head. It's all beginning to fit. Ryan checked out Lauren's Paradise High musical connections, but I bet it never occurred to him to look at the choirmaster of Little Falls Academy.

"It was Laurence's idea that they take on 'The Flower Duet' in the first place," Paul continues, looking down at his fine-boned hands. "I doubt Gerard, with his pedestrian tastes—popular musicals, oratory, and the like"—he practically shudders—"would have thought to give such challenging material to a couple of high school kids from the sticks. Jennifer probably caught the opera bug off Laurence as a child—he's been a friend of the family forever. If he's somehow involved in this, it's going to break their hearts all over again—"

"Well, thanks for your help," I cut in, my mind leaping ahead to how much new stuff I have to tell Ryan. I wonder if he'll be pleased. It's disgusting how much I need his approval. I hardly recognize myself, and that's saying a lot.

"You've really clarified some things for me," I add, shouldering Carmen's backpack. I shoot Paul a grateful smile, prepare to leave.

"Hey, you sure about that coffee?" he says with easy charm. "No time like the present. I can call the Daleys —Louisa knows me well—run you home afterward. We have a lot to cover. I can start getting in touch with all the best schools, get the trustees talking about you."

I feel that strange discomfort again, as if Carmen's trying to tell me something.

Paul's face is open, and there's nothing sleazy about his body language. Unlike Gerard Masson and Laurence Barry, he doesn't even try to touch me. Or hold me to a promise. In fact, he turns and tidies up his things while he waits for my answer.

"You have a remarkable voice, Carmen," he says gently. "You're very young. And Fiona Fellows seems to have a . . . *blind spot* where you're concerned, doesn't realize the treasure she's been sitting on. Probably literally, the way she talks about you. . . ."

The stitch in my side flares more painfully still.

"I don't think you've been made aware of all your options," he continues, snapping his messenger bag shut before turning to face me. "I've got links to the best music faculties in the country. That's all this is about. I'm not like Gerard Masson, with his stupid little crushes and extra practice sessions. I've been at the receiving end of that kind of thing myself, and it's the last thing I'd do to you. This is purely about your *future*."

For a moment I feel dizzy. Should I go with him or go find Ryan? *Lauren or Carmen?* The disembodied pounding in my side intensifies, like something torn.

When I still don't say anything, Paul raises an inquiring eyebrow.

I shake my head, knowing any normal girl in my position would accept in a heartbeat. But that's just it. *I'm sorry, Carmen, but I'm batting for Lauren.* And for me.

"Uh, thanks, but I'm good," I reply. "Got things to do tonight."

"Rain check?" Paul says good-naturedly. He straightens up, stretches elegantly. "Though you seem like a smart girl—I'm sure you've figured it all out already."

"You bet," I say, giving him a stupid girly wave over my shoulder as I leave, hoping it seems natural. Not believing he means any of it for a second.

It's dark by the time I make my way back from the lockers and head across the Paradise High parking lot, pulling Carmen's hood up to hide my profile from the breeze, and from curious eyes. I notice Paul Stenborg herding the last of his charges onto the bus bound for Port Marie. He doesn't give me a second glance as I pass under a nearby streetlight and head for the pedestrian gate next to the school's main driveway.

I wonder where Laurence Barry is, and what he's doing. *Tonight*, I think, *we'll see what you're hiding down there, old man.*

I pull the edges of Carmen's hood forward even more, turn up the collar on her denim jacket, and start threading my way across town; peer into the windows of the family restaurants on main street, the town's only video rental store. And I think about Ryan constantly, even look forward to eating his mother's strangely tasteless but immaculately presented cooking, in awkward silence because he might be at the table, close enough to touch. If I can bring myself to do it.

I walk slowly, enjoying the faint tang of salt in the air. Even the sounds of dogs going berserk in their front yards as I pass by just makes me smile. I don't know how long I have, and, for once, I don't want it to end. Though it isn't the kind of boy-meets-girl scenario anyone in their right mind would wish for. You have to take it as it comes, I guess.

And then, within sight of Ryan's street, I feel a light pressure on the back of my neck, a small sting, and I go down.

CHAPTER 22

When I wake, it's dark. So dark at first that my eyes have trouble making out anything. I'm on my side, facing a wall. There's a heavy weight around my neck, unaccustomed pressure.

I think maybe I fainted on the footpath, and I'm having difficulties focusing, but then I'm hit by a wave of smells so strong I gag out loud. Human waste, old food, rust, bleach, mold, blood. Layered over the top of each other, the air so fetid and soupy I can taste it on my tongue.

And I'm lying on something coarse. It creaks when I shift my free arm experimentally, lift my head an inch or two. A cot?

There's breathing in here, not mine. The sound of a clock ticking.

"You okay?" someone whispers. It's a girl.

For a minute, I wonder if I've fallen out of Carmen's life into a new one. Where *am* I? What am I doing here?

I try to sit up, and discover the weight around my neck is some kind of iron collar. I follow the chain with my hands to find it padlocked to a metal cleat in the wall behind me. There isn't much room to move once I sit up. And I've caught sight of that faint, telltale luminosity coming off my skin, so I stay facing the wall. I don't want to freak out whoever's in here with me. They've probably got enough to deal with already.

In my head, I am able to run, in order, through the full Latin verse that Mahler set to music over one hundred years ago, and backward through every single thing that I have done since the bus from St. Joseph's first drew up in the parking lot of Paradise High, and I know that Carmen Zappacosta and I are not yet done. *All* the details are still there. Clear and sharp and immediately accessible. So where am I?

Ryan! I think suddenly, my breathing quickening. I was supposed to meet him. What will he be thinking?

It's like I fell into a rabbit hole between the school and his place.

I feel for my general shape in the dark, and I recognize the same denim jacket I put on this morning over the same hooded sweatshirt, Carmen's improbably narrow, little-boy jeans. The same dirty canvas sneakers. Carmen's bag is gone, along with her sparkly wallet, her mobile phone, and her music, but I've already committed that to memory anyway, and earthly possessions seem the least of my troubles. I glance quickly through the hair hanging down over my right shoulder. It, too, seems the same. Curly. Long. Dense. Almost too heavy for my head.

Through my screen of wild curls I make out two shapes in the darkness on different sides of the room, both with long, straight hair—one big, one tiny, like a bird girl. The taller one is visibly trembling, as if she is dangerously close to hypothermia. The small one is so still she might be made of stone. Though it should be too dark for me to make out their features, I can see them as clearly as if the sun is shining overhead, and I know who they are. And I can make out the dimensions of the room, too, which is bare save for a staircase in the far corner. Like the staircase in Ryan's dream.

Like their faces, I've seen this room before.

"You get used to it," says the bird girl quietly. Her voice is dry, like fallen leaves. It sounds almost rusty, like she hasn't used it much lately. Except maybe to scream.

I try to reconcile the outline of the smaller girl with the photos from her dresser. She looks beaten, emaciated, unlovely. Her ash blond hair seems white to my eyes, even in this light.

"Lauren?" I ask, though I don't need to, nausea in my words. The smell in here is so strong, it's crowding my thoughts, the very oxygen out of the room.

"Who wants to know?" she replies. Her voice is thin and uninterested.

"Ignore her," pleads the taller figure, Jennifer. "She doesn't seem to care if we ever get out! Does anyone else know we're here? Please say yes." She is speaking barely above a low whisper, but she might as well be screaming; fear crowds the spaces between her words.

"Her brother does," I say, hoping my voice sounds reassuring. "We were supposed to come back here tonight, to try and get you both out. But something happened on my way back from Paradise High before I could meet up with him. Any idea what that was?"

A chemical taste rises in my mouth, and I have to

stop to vomit over the side of the bed. So much for never getting sick. I face the wall again, gasping, waiting for the unfamiliar nausea to subside.

Ryan, I think miserably. *I found them. Now what do I do?*

Like an unconscious echo, Lauren gasps aloud, "Ryan?" and she begins to cry.

It is like a dam bursting, and a chill flash breaks out across my skin. Lauren sounds inhuman, like a wounded animal, and across the room Jennifer shifts uncomfortably on her metal cot.

There's a sudden loud banging on the door above us, at the top of the stairs, and Lauren's crying cuts off abruptly as if she's been choked.

"Don't make me come down and hurt you, Lauren!" a man's voice bellows. So distorted with anger I can't tell whether I've heard it before. Lauren gives a tiny whimper and lies down. Her cot shifts and creaks.

Jennifer and I are silent for a while, and then we start talking again, as though the other girl isn't lying there, facedown and rigid, listening to every word we say with every cell in her body.

"Did he hurt you?" I ask Jennifer fiercely. I dart

a quick glance in her direction. She's still trembling uncontrollably.

"Apart from ripping some hair out of my scalp because I wouldn't do what he wanted, and sticking a needle in my neck, no," she whispers. "I'm still in one piece. But I'm so *scared*."

"He hasn't had the time to do anything yet," I say. "He's been greedy with the two of us. Snatching us so close together."

"So far, all he wants me to do is *sing*," the girl continues, puzzlement in her voice. "But I think he's a little . . . disappointed."

"That's good," I reassure her. And it is. I'm relieved. He's had her for almost a week, and all he's done is ask her to perform a few tunes? "That's great. You're okay. Hold on to that."

"There's a room just up the stairs," Jennifer adds, her voice growing a little stronger. "With a piano in it. A baby grand. Candle holders. A gold music stand. Armchairs. Like a recital room. He keeps it real tidy. That's where he takes me when I'm not here. Sometimes he takes *her* instead."

I look over quickly. Jennifer inclines her head in

Lauren's direction in the dark, forgetting I shouldn't be able to see, though of course I can.

I hear the other girl draw a sharp breath. Force myself to leave her alone a while longer, though I have so many questions. She's not ready to talk. She may never be ready.

"He just looks at you?" I say in Jennifer's direction. "When he makes you sing?"

"He says that he was always obsessed with me, but I've changed. I'm not the girl he remembers. I've *defiled* his memories of me, even though my voice is better, stronger, than it ever was. Things can change a lot in two years." There's a shudder in Jennifer's rich, expressive voice. Her words tumble out so quickly I can barely make sense of them. "He said I left town before he could act on it, that he shouldn't have hesitated before, but he's been waiting for me to come back ever since. And the minute I did . . . I shouldn't have opened the door. I just wasn't expecting to see him there, so late.

"Plus, I'd had a crush on him forever—it all came rushing back, and that didn't help. I didn't know he was some kind of . . . pervert. I wasn't thinking. I was kind of . . . *flattered* he remembered me." She sounds disgusted with herself.

I wrinkle my forehead in the dark. A *crush?* *Flattered?* Out of the corner of my eye I see Lauren sit up suddenly, pushing her long hair back from her face with shaking hands.

"I only came back because my aunt insisted I sing at Julia's wedding," Jennifer says. "So who else knows we're here?" The hope in her voice is painful to hear.

"Just me and Ryan," I say, my back to them both, still facing the wall. "But he should be on his way right now." I sound more confident than I feel. "He knows where we are. We'd planned to get you out of the basement tonight, anyway. He'll just have to get started on his own. We just have to wait a while, and we'll be free. Simple as that."

"That's fantastic," Jennifer murmurs, relief flooding her voice, though she cannot stop shaking. "So fantastic. I keep thinking I've stumbled into someone's idea of a sick joke. Though he did say something strange before I passed out. Said it was a shame I'd gotten so big and so . . . fat." There's indignation in her tone.

That makes me frown. Something familiar in it.

"Said he liked me much better when I was smaller," Jennifer says incredulously. "Like *her*, I suppose." In the dark, I see her wave vaguely in Lauren's direction.

I hear Lauren inhale sharply, and I reach the same terrible conclusion a heartbeat after she does.

"You mean," Lauren says in a trembling tone, "all this time I've been here because of . . . of *you*? Like some substitute for *you*? He couldn't have you, so he took *me*?" Her voice flies up the scale, breaks sharply on the last word.

"You don't know that," I say, but she's right. The timing is too awful, the coincidence too awful. Just over two years ago, both girls were bird-bright, tiny, center stage together for one mesmerizing performance. Two rare sopranos brimming with talent. Then one flew the nest and the other was swiftly . . . caged.

Lauren begins to wail. "Do you KNOW what he's DONE to me?"

She's suddenly uncaring of whether the monster above us can hear as she mercilessly catalogues the sins that have been perpetrated against her since she was taken. As she speaks, her voice drops lower and lower, grows mechanical.

In between the retelling of inexorable hours that felt like months, months that felt like lifetimes stitched together end to end, every sordid, unclean thing, I can hear Jennifer's harsh sobs.

"I'm sorry," she cries, over and over, hands covering her face. "I'm so sorry."

"He says it's to keep me *safe*," Lauren murmurs. "That he's the only person who can truly appreciate my . . . talent."

Though I am moved almost beyond bearing, I remain dry-eyed, my forehead resting against the wall. It is a peculiar thing, though *I* cannot cry tears, the body I'm in may choose to follow a different directive. I am grateful for the darkness because I need not fake them.

"Last year," Lauren whispers, "when I refused to sing once, he hit me so hard that I nearly died. And, you know," she says, her voice suddenly fierce, "I was almost *glad*. I've been in hell," she says simply. "Am in hell. And now you are, too."

Jennifer weeps noisily, and I am reminded of Lauren's mother, completely undone by grief. I imagine Lauren, doubled over alone in this room, and something rises up in me like a red fog. For a minute I cannot see, and my head is filled with a terrible roaring, like the sound a city makes when it is being razed, stone by stone, to the ground. There is a firestorm in me, greater than me. I almost cannot contain it.

I don't hear Jennifer's question. She repeats it sharply. "Where *are* we? Where has he taken us?"

"You're not that far from home, Jennifer," I reply distantly, blood still in my eyes, roaring in my ears. A great tempest inside. "You're at his place, Laurence Barry's place. We're going to get you out."

"But I don't understand." There is confusion in Jennifer's voice. "Laurence Barry? Are they in this together?"

"Who?" I say, confusion in mine now. "Who's in this together?"

Then Lauren begins to laugh, and the sound is so strange that I feel that cold flash race across the surface of Carmen's skin again. "We're going to die here," she crows, rocking backward and forward on her makeshift bed. "We'll die here, and no one will find us until we're bones."

Her crazy laughter grows into a wordless keening, until the banging from above starts again. The shrieking ceases instantly, Lauren making herself as small as possible on her metal cot. Somehow, the sudden silence is almost worse.

When Lauren's voice finally issues out of the darkness again, it's muffled and flat and weirdly controlled.

"Ryan's not coming, no one's coming," she says. "Because this isn't Laurence Barry's place."

I freeze, unable to believe we were wrong.

"It's Paul Stenborg's. *Sten-borg*. Get it? *Stone fortress*. We're *never* going to get out."

CHAPTER
23

Right dream, wrong place.

I react so strongly to her words that I forget and turn away from the wall. *Paul's place?* How is that possible?

Both girls rear back from me so powerfully that I curse aloud. It's too late to hide.

Now they can see me as clearly as I have seen them all along. For a moment, I recall the shining man, my dream brother. How his light pierced the darkness as if he were a little sun. Do I seem like that to them, trapped all these days in darkness?

"It's okay," I say wildly. "It's nothing."

"Who *are* you?" Jennifer chokes out.

"*What* are you?" breathes Lauren.

It's a good question, the very question I'd like an answer to myself, only, it's as if the word, the name, for what *I* truly am has been cut from my mind. Always, when I reach for it, when it should be obvious, it's not there.

I'm desperate to set their minds at ease as much as the situation allows, but there's that little problem of trust that I seem to have, and I'm silent for a long time; weighing up the pros and cons, I think you call it. Only in a situation like this one, there are no cons. There's nothing left to lose. I could die in this stupidly frail, borrowed body and never know the answer, never make any meaningful human contact, and that's not what I want. What I *want* is to talk to someone so badly, tell someone about *me*—the real me and not the face I'm presenting to the world—that my misgivings suddenly disappear and I wonder why I held onto them for so long.

So I tell them almost everything of myself that I have managed to piece together in *this* lifetime, and of the multitude of disjointed lifetimes that I only dimly recall living. I speak so fast, my words falling over each other in the rush to get out, that I'm sure I'm making no sense at all—

"And I can see things," I hear myself say, "about people. Some people I don't even need to touch to know what's eating away at their . . . souls. I just know—"

I'm just grateful for the chance to tell my story because then it might now stay, and I might now remember.

For a while, they cleave to the sound of my voice and forget the unspeakable place we have found ourselves in, and they shower me with questions.

"So is she in there, then? Carmen?" Lauren asks in awe.

"And can she hear you, Mercy?" says Jennifer, her voice uncertain, a person who has always dealt in concrete realities.

"Yes, she is," I say carefully. "And she probably can hear me. But I'm not really sure whether she knows what's going on. I hope she doesn't. It's almost like she's sleepwalking, I suppose. She's a soprano, you know, like you are. But tiny, Lauren's size. With dark hair."

There is no need for me to say this—they can see her now—but what is inside me feels so removed from what is outside that I must make the divergence clear.

"We're his type," says Lauren in a small voice. "I think he's . . . *collecting* us. *Treasuring* us."

And I know she's right. Paul said so himself, was talking about himself by the piano after last night's rehearsal, only I didn't know it. Didn't grasp the underlying darkness in his words.

"Does Ryan know? About the real you, I mean," Lauren asks, resting her chin on her drawn-up knees.

I hesitate for a moment, before saying, "No. But he suspects I'm not altogether, uh . . . *normal*."

Both girls laugh quietly.

"Does . . . Paul?" asks Jennifer. She swallows jerkily before she can say his name.

"I'm not sure," I reply. "I think I was under a streetlight when he grabbed me. Things probably happened so fast he never even noticed. I'm not sure the fact that I glow in the dark would change anything."

"Make you more or less . . . collectible, you mean," Lauren whispers.

"So what else can you . . . do?" Jennifer says, her voice husky from crying.

"I'm not sure," I say slowly. "Sing."

"We can all sing," says Lauren disgustedly. "That's what got us into trouble in the first place. I'm never going to do it again, if I get out of here. *Never*."

"No one will be able to stop me," Jennifer disagrees fiercely.

"Who knows if I'll still be able to . . . after all this," I say.

I don't tell them about being able to see in the dark like a cat, or make random impersonations of complete strangers. I don't want them to feel self-conscious, and I don't quite believe the last part myself. It might have been some kind of fluke, a shared auditory hallucination, a temporary madness. Without any explanation or context for it, I'm not going to class it as some kind of . . . gift.

The three of us are silent for a long time.

"If we ever get out of here," Lauren suddenly says, urgently, "you have to promise you'll tell Ryan? He'll want to know. But he won't believe me. It's got to come from you."

The links of my chain lie cold and heavy against my heart as I draw my knees up under my chin. "Oh, he'll believe you," I say softly. "He's believed you when everyone else gave up a long time ago. He's put everything on hold in his life just to find you. He doesn't think about doing anything else. He *heard* you, kept hearing you when even your parents . . ." I don't bother finishing my sentence. She's been hurt enough, no need to spell it out. "Anyway, it's remarkable. *He's* remarkable."

"You like him," Lauren says softly after a pause. It's a statement, not a question.

"*I* like him," I agree quietly. "But Carmen won't know him from Adam when I'm gone. Which could be any time now. I have a habit of just . . . flitting away. It will only confuse things. So if he doesn't know, don't tell him."

Then the door above the staircase is thrown wide, and I am rendered momentarily blind by the brilliant light from the overhead fluorescents being turned on, like the heavens are opening.

"Ladies," Paul Stenborg says conversationally, shutting and locking the door behind him, pocketing the key.

I have always hated that term, feel an unreasonable rage when it is directed at me personally. Especially now. My left hand begins to ache dully.

Jennifer and Lauren moan into their fingers, their sensitive eyes screwed tight against the unnatural illumination. Carmen's pupils have contracted to mere pinpoints, but my adjustment to the light is almost instantaneous.

The room reveals its dingy secrets. There are rust-colored marks on the floor, on the walls, buckets containing human waste in one corner, food scraps everywhere, empty bottles of cleaning fluid, water, rubbish, rags. I look up at the man descending the staircase, strolling down unaffectedly in his designer shirtsleeves. Then to the other two girls, chained by their necks to their respective walls, as I am.

Jennifer looks whole and largely unmarked by her ordeal, as I'd expected. Her round face, glossy hair, and smooth skin shine with rude health. But Lauren is a ghost girl, with cracked lips, sunken eyes, collapsed cheeks, a paper-white skin marked with random scars. Her hair, long and matted, *is* more white than blond. It has fallen out in places, so I can see down to her pale scalp. She will never be beautiful again, and is so dangerously thin that her feet, head, and hands seem too big for her body.

She cringes from the illumination, hands laced tightly over her eyes, her mouth a terrified arc, her fear palpable. *It hangs about her like a detectable odor, a familiar on her shoulder, gnawing at her flesh.*

I have already felt an echo of this fear through Ryan's skin, how the dark is almost more bearable to her than the light. Bad things happen in the light. Bad things are about to happen now; one needs no second sight to know it. The pain in my hand spreads up my forearm like wildfire, and I feel the sweat suddenly stand out on Carmen's brow, her heart frantically pounding.

I put my head down as Paul walks among us, studying us curiously as if we are museum exhibits.

Jennifer is dressed like Lauren is, as I am, in a short-sleeved nightgown, and I see that her glasses are missing, that her nose is heavily freckled, and that she is voluptuous, tall, everything an opera singer should be. Paul runs a hand up one of Jennifer's long pale calves, causing Lauren to moan and rock on her fold-out bed.

When Jennifer reacts violently to his touch, Paul's response is immediate and brutal, and so is the flowering wound above Jennifer's eye.

"You'll learn," he says quietly, unwrapping Jennifer's chain from around his fist and crossing the room to where Lauren cringes and moans louder.

"Lauren was a slow learner," he murmurs, squeezing

her small face in the fingers of one hand until she bares her teeth reluctantly, like a cornered animal. "And you see what happens?"

Jennifer screams again and looks away, blood still running freely down the side of her face.

Tears leak slowly out of Lauren's eyes and over Paul's long fingers. I study the terrible damage to her shattered mouth. I have seen faces like hers before, I remember now, dimly, in war zones, or caused by old age and disease. Not like this; never like this. Violence and pleasure the same impulse.

The anger rises in me again, so fiercely that Carmen's heart skips a beat in her chest, and there is that twinge again, only stronger now, as if Carmen is waking up, is struggling to be heard. I don't want her to see this, or to remember. No one so innocent, so young, should have to.

I jam my burning left hand beneath my right in agony, and the slight movement causes my chain to rattle. Paul turns his head sharply at the sound, releases Lauren's ruined face from his grip. I see the marks his fingers made, a starker white against her already stark skin.

"You," he says over his shoulder to Jennifer, still

sobbing, "got too gross. Too fleshy for my liking. It was a shock when you opened the door. I was offended when I saw how much you'd changed, although I was already committed. This one," and I know he means me, "is how you once were. But so much better—a rare creature, a pearl beyond price, all for me."

He steps forward and lifts my chin gently.

"Sing, Carmen," he says kindly, as if we are standing together in the empty assembly hall at Paradise High, beside the upright piano. The youthful, handsome teacher; the wise-cracking student. "Sing and show them why I had to have you, why you are so peerless."

He caresses my face, and it is as if he has put a hot iron to it. I jerk away from his touch, and the instinctive gesture of rejection obliterates the beauty from his features in an instant. He lifts me by the chain around my neck, and I am off my feet, hanging before him like a rag doll. We are eye to burning eye.

He shakes me. "Sing!" he hisses, the Devil in his voice. "Sing or suffer."

"Please," gasps Lauren.

"Do it," Jennifer begs.

I have no sense of up or down, so dizzy that the

world has telescoped. *I* am the world, or the world is in me, and in me so much rage and fear and loathing. I can feel plates moving, floes breaking, separation, reconfiguration, an unlinking.

And the pain in my hand, my forearm, burns so fiercely that I let out a shattering scream that has Paul staggering to his knees, clutching at his ears. The two girls on either side of the room rock backward on their cots, holding their heads at the sonic after-bite.

I fall to the floor at the end of my taut chain. Cradling my burning hand against my chest, leaning on my right, on my knees, panting like a dying animal.

As a thin trickle of blood seeps from between Paul's fingers, I feel something inside me splitting in two, hear gasps from the others, dim shapes above me to the left and right. In that instant, I catch Carmen's slight figure fall away, forwards onto the floor. Her body lies there, lifelessly, at my feet as I rise and bellow:

> *Si dextra manus tua scandalizat te,*
> *abscide eam!*
> *Quod si oculus tuus dexter scandalizat te, erue*
> *eum!*

I have no sense of my physical self, but I know that I am very tall. Six, maybe seven, feet.

My perspective has changed. The room that once reeked of the cavernous dark can almost no longer hold me. Its dimensions feel doll-like, unreal.

And I know this too, because I watch their eyes follow me upward, huge in their white faces, until I am standing over Paul Stenborg and I am his horizon, I am his world, and the fear in him is as a detectable odor, a familiar on his shoulder, gnawing at his flesh, and it is *good*.

"Who are you?" he shrieks, blood still trickling from each shattered eardrum.

"I am *pain*, Paul," I whisper, a whisper to rend steel, to rend stone, a whisper to wake even the dead. "The living sword. And I shall gather all things that offend, all those that do iniquity, and I shall cast them into a furnace of fire."

The words come from me freely, as if they have waited all these lifetimes to emerge.

I am dimly aware of Jennifer's cries, Lauren's terrified whimpering.

And I raise Paul Stenborg by the collar of his shirt,

high, high above the ground, with a fist like bloody chain mail, and shake him as he shook Carmen's frail, small frame, and I say again:

"*Si dextra manus tua scandalizat te, abscide eam.* If your hand causes you to sin, Paul, cut it off. *Quod si oculus tuus dexter scandalizat te, erue eum.* And if your eye causes you to sin, Paul, pluck it out."

And with my burning left hand, I put out his eyes, first one and then the other, so that he may never see again, may never covet another living being for the rest of his days. See not music nor color, joy, rage, or fear. His no longer. Willingly given, willingly taken away. I to do it. And it is done.

For I am the living sword and a creature of my word. The words come to me, and I know them to be the truth. Whatever I did to set the sorry course of my life in tremulous motion all those years ago, these things I know now to be immutable.

"And there shall be a wailing," I say quietly, setting the man gently upon his feet, "a gnashing of teeth."

As Paul Stenborg staggers around his basement fortress screaming and roaring, blood streaming from his ears, from the wounds his eyes once were, I move toward first Lauren, then Jennifer, and rip their bonds out of the wall with my bare hands.

Lastly, I do the same for my poor Carmen, and carry her lifeless body up the stairs, through a stinking warren of underground rooms and shield doors the monster has built beneath the floor of his home. And on into the clean darkness beyond Paul Stenborg's back door, Lauren and Jennifer following behind me as swiftly as their chains and their injuries will allow.

And the starlight in my eyes, the infinite sky, the cold wind that lifts the hair of my head, each strand straight, even, and exactly the same. . . . That is all I remember, for a time.

CHAPTER
24

I am facedown against the cold, sweet-smelling grass. It is night. There is soil beneath Carmen's curled hands, her curling black hair. And Lauren's urgent voice is in our ears before I can think to rise.

It is no dream, I think, momentarily disappointed. I am not asleep. Luc will not appear this time, either to praise or to damn me depending upon his mood.

I am so tired. So strangely tired I can barely open my eyes, but her words make me stiffen.

"Jennifer's gone to get help," she says urgently. "The story is that Carmen distracted Paul long enough to enable us all to get away. Carmen's going to be a hero, Mercy. Because you can't be. Can you hear me?"

"His eyes?" I mumble, getting to my knees slowly, the world righting itself once more along its proper axis.

The night is kinder to Lauren. She seems almost her own self in the moonlight; the girl from the photos, dispensing hugs to a thousand friends. And I wonder if she could be that girl again. In this moment, it seems almost possible.

"It all happened so fast that we can't be sure," she says confidently, as if she is reciting the truth.

We hear sirens in the distance, voices approaching, a crowd, lights bearing down on where Lauren sits with one arm fast around Carmen's thin shoulders.

"Carmen woke from some kind of drugged sleep," she says, "went crazy, hit out, threw bleach around . . ."

My senses are sharpening all the time. It could work. If you were stupid enough, and willing to believe anything you heard.

"And the monster?" I ask.

"Still locked in his own cellar," Lauren says with grim celebration as the first of our flashlight-bearing rescue party spies us and lets out a shout. "Be brave and stick to the story," she adds as she stands up unsteadily and waves one thin arm in the air. "Over here!" she cries.

She looks down at me and grins, and for a second I have to look away from her shattered mouth. "But I don't need to tell you that. You've done a great job of protecting yourself so far."

"Oh my God!" cries someone in the distance. Voices grow in volume as many people begin to run toward us. "*Who* is that?"

"Can you see who it is?"

"I think it's Lauren! Lauren Daley! She's alive!"

And we are suddenly engulfed by a wave of people, a tidal wave of human emotion.

"We're free!" Lauren whispers with elation as she is borne away from me. "Free at last!"

But not you, beats my borrowed heart, my traitor heart. *Not you. For you, a different fate.*

Now there are arms lifting me. Lights both red and blue; a stretcher waiting; sheets taut, crisp, and white. "You're safe," murmurs someone kindly as I am passed from hand to hand. "You're safe."

I am covered with a blanket, shielded from the advancing media, separated from the others so that our stories may be cross-checked and verified. But we will hold true, we will hold fast. And I think wearily, *Let them come. Let them break against us as a wave.*

So tired. I close my eyes, content to sleep the sleep of the untroubled for a while. For this time, I have earned it.

"Mercy?" His voice is familiar, pleading, and I frown. There's that weight upon my eyelids, snaking along my limbs. I have never felt so earthbound, so heavy.

"Luc?" I mutter. "Why can't I see you?"

I feel him take one of my hands in his, and the corners of my mouth lift involuntarily at his touch. I'd know it anywhere. The bass note of my messed-up existence.

"So good to have you back," I murmur leadenly. "So good to be back."

His grip tightens and I frown, beginning to feel a flowering of contact. Luc has *never* been an open book to me. It has always been part of his allure. What has changed?

"They told me I had to let you rest, but I couldn't wait," he says urgently. "I slipped past the security guards, the night nurse—they'll kill me if they find me here. But Lauren told me the most incredible story. Is it true? Who's Luke?" His voice is both eager and sullen.

I withdraw my hands as if burned, and the feeling of something being laid open is abruptly cut off. The words are incomprehensible to me, as if they have been spoken out of order, or in Old English. Or French.

"Why can't I open my eyes?" I say, struggling to sit up. "Who are you?"

But I am tethered to a bed by a battery of tubes and pipes, and the feeling of being chained again makes me roar and flail until the electronic beeping that stands for my heart becomes a wailing alarm.

"Shit!" he says. "It's just *me*, Carmen, Mercy. Jesus!"

A door slams quickly. Another opens.

"Code Blue!" exclaims a voice. "She's flatlining!"

There is a rush of fevered activity around me. The sound of hurrying feet in soft-soled shoes.

"I am *not* flatlining," I say angrily. "There's something wrong with your machine." And as I say the words, my heart rate falls and falls and falls until a steady, even beeping resumes. "You see?" I say calmly, palms lying outward and open on the bed.

I cannot open my eyes, but I know the room is full of people standing over me. Their consternation is obvious to me, even without my sight. I feel it, like warm crosscurrents mingling in the air above my head.

"Are you in pain, child?" a woman asks worriedly, checking my pulse.

I have trouble moving my head from side to side, but I still do it. "No, but I can't open my eyes," I growl.

The woman lets go of my wrist, and the pain in my left hand subsides, the building pressure behind my eyes fading away before her inner life can be exposed to me.

Someone else laughs gently. "That would be because we gave you enough midazolam to knock out a horse. I can't understand why she's still awake and able to string a sentence together, Doris. It's unprecedented."

"Well, she's a tough one," a different man suggests gruffly. "So give her a little more. She needs to sleep. She's already done four hours of police interviews, and they've got a press conference lined up for tomorrow morning. And replace that EKG! It has to be faulty. A heart rate like that couldn't have been possible. I mean, look at her."

Electrodes are swiftly disconnected, then the machine is wheeled away, another connected in its place. The same even beeping resumes.

"You see?" says a new voice with satisfaction.

There is a small sting in my arm. From a change in the air, I know that several people have left the room.

"Rest now," another woman says gently as she shuts the door behind her.

After several minutes, the other door opens.

"Just don't upset me," I warn raggedly.

"I didn't mean to scare you," Ryan whispers, and it *is* Ryan, I realize it now. His hand seeks mine again on the bed covers, our fingers interlacing. "But I needed to hear it for myself, from you."

In his touch, I discern a faint riot of feeling, of color. Different this time; not burning, but soft, like the afterglow before nightfall. There's curiosity, affection, relief. Love? It has a little of that nature to it. But love for whom? For Lauren? For me?

So tired. So tired, I don't even react when he holds my small hand up to his cheekbone, runs it along his jawline, before placing it down again, gently. Our fingers still entwined. Every girl's dream, and I can't lift my eyelids to focus on his heartbreaking face.

"We don't know how to thank you," he breathes reverently. "For giving her back to us. When you never

REBECCA LIM

came home, I knew I'd done that to you, placed you in *his* way somehow. That I'd got it all horribly wrong. And when I thought you could be dead, too . . ."

For a moment he doesn't speak, and on my hand I feel a warm salt tear. And in it, all the horror.

"For me?" I sigh, making little sense. For I am sinking like a stone, a cut anchor.

"Is it true?" he says, wonder in his voice. "What Lauren told me?"

I want to nod, but I can't seem to move my head. It doesn't feel as if it belongs to me any more, or is even on temporary loan. The bonds between Carmen and me are dissolving, and this time, for the first time, I can feel it. The two of us no longer a unit, becoming two separate beings, even as Ryan watches over us, oblivious to the seismic shift.

"The midazolam," I say with difficulty, though it is not only that. "No time."

And I know he must bend close to hear my voice, for I smell the faint salt sweat of him for an instant, feel his sweet breath on her forehead.

He clasps my hand harder. "Tomorrow," he says brightly, "we'll talk tomorrow. They'll have to throw me out to get me to leave. I want to hear all of it. Everything. It's been torture, not knowing. My parents, they don't know what to say, what to do. Neither do I. There aren't any words, enough words."

When I don't answer, he murmurs, "We were right, you know, it was the place, the church. Only heard from the perspective of Stenborg's place, not Barry's. Stenborg's house *backs* onto part of the church grounds." His grip tightens on mine. "He had a prior conviction for stalking," he says darkly. "Something he conveniently whited out when he applied for the job at Port Marie. No one bothered to run a background police check because his resume was so extraordinary. The Framlingham School's partly to blame—they didn't tell Port Marie he was a psychopath because it would have looked bad for them. She was one of his students with an extraordinary soprano voice. Sound familiar? He sent her thousands of dirty text messages, even climbed in her bedroom window one night. They found him in the girl's bed, naked. Her mother took out a restraining order, so he left before the school could sack him, and started over. Spread around the story that it was the girl who stalked him, when all along it was the other way around."

278

I frown weakly, losing the train of his words. Something is different this time. Something happened to me, down there, in the monster's pit. As we unraveled, I almost felt the point where she ended and I began. Maybe, if I am displaced another time, and a time after that, I will be able to find that space, that fork in the road, again and again, until I find my true self, standing at the end of it.

And there's something else. I am leaving, and this time *I know it.*

I have never had warning before, never had certainty. But this time, I am so sure that I rear up suddenly, like Lazarus, like Frankenstein's monster, a drowning person grasping at a spar on the ocean.

Ryan pulls back, startled. Still blind, I grab at his shirtfront with what remains of *us.*

"Tomorrow," I whisper, my voice like something carried back on the wind from the afterlife, "Carmen may not remember what's happened. She may not remember *you*, or your parents. She may have no recollection of Jennifer, or even of Lauren, or of her time here before today. You must protect her. See her home safe. Maintain the fiction. Keep me secret. Her future turns on it, and her future is *bright.*"

"Why are you telling me this?" Ryan says confusedly as he braces me against him.

"Going," I murmur. "Into someone else, to *be* someone else. Not here. Not with you."

I feel that sense of loosening quicken, like sparks flying upward on a cold morning.

"How do I find you again?" Ryan says desperately, shaking Carmen, shaking *me* even further free of my moorings.

I sigh. "You can't. Could be anywhere, anyone. No time."

I touch his face with Carmen's cold fingers. Kiss him once, gently.

"No! Mercy," Ryan cries, crushing *her* closer, not knowing I am already gone. "Mercy!"

And I watch from above as Carmen's breathing evens out in sleep, and find myself falling out of her life, into another. . . .